D0563623

The Secret Diary of Sarah Chamberlain

The Secret Diary of Sarah Chamberlain

SARAH NORKUS

LIVING
INK
BOOKS
Writing Worth Reading®

The Secret Diary of Sarah Chamberlain
Copyright © 2012 by Sarah Norkus
Published by Living Ink Books, an imprint of
AMG Publishers, Inc.
6815 Shallowford Rd.
Chattanooga, Tennessee 37421

All rights reserved. Except for brief quotations in printed
reviews, no part of this publication may be reproduced,
stored in a retrieval system, or transmitted in any form or
by any means (printed, written, photocopied, visual elec-
tronic, audio, or otherwise) without the prior permission of
the publisher.

This is a work of fiction. Names, characters, places, and
incidents either are the product of the author's imagination or are used fictitiously. Any resemblance to actual
persons, either living or dead, events, or locales is entirely
coincidental.

First Printing—June 2012

Print edition   ISBN 13: 978-0-89957-770-8
EPUB edition   ISBN 13: 978-1-61715-307-5
Mobi edition   ISBN 13: 978-1-61715-308-2
ePDF edition   ISBN 13: 978-1-61715-309-9

Published in association with the
Harvey Literary Agency, Dunwoody, GA

Cover layout and design by
Garborg Design Works, Savage, MN

Interior design and typesetting by Kristin Goble at
PerfecType, Nashville, TN

Edited by Kathy Ide and Rick Steele

Printed in the United States of America

17 16 15 14 13 12 –B– 6 5 4 3 2 1

Coming Soon
from author Sarah Norkus
and Living Ink Books

The Secret Treasure of Battersea

Chapter One

Saturday, June 14, 2008

Em stomped her foot in frustration as she watched her mom disappear down the attic stairs to answer the door. Her eyes widened in surprise. She looked down; her right foot stood at an angle an inch above her left. She inched her foot back, revealing a wooden slat no longer flush with the floor.

Em dragged the three-legged table she had been left to balance back to its original position against the wall. Kneeling down, Em hooked her fingers over the end of the slat and tugged. The slat rose about six inches. Em looked down into the empty hole, but could see nothing in the blackness. She slid her hand into the cavity and jerked back when her fingers touched something soft.

Lying flat on the floor, Em peered into the hole and promptly sneezed from the dust she had stirred up. She absently rubbed a finger across her nose, then reached in again, more cautiously this time. Em's hand curled around a small, fabric-wrapped bundle. She pulled it out into the dim light from the dormer window.

A strange tingle raced up her spine as she stared at the little parcel. She wrestled with herself about the right thing to do. She was in the Petersburg Ladies Benevolent Society House. Everything in the house was the property of the society. She knew she should give it to her mother, as the president of the society, but her excitement over the find was overwhelming.

She unfolded the piece of cloth. Inside was a book about three by five inches. The brown leather cover was rough and pebbly under the finger she trailed across the cover. Embossed in gold across the middle were the words *My Diary*. The edges of it had small cracks, but otherwise, it seemed to be in good shape. Em gently opened the book to the first page, which had yellowed with age. Written in faded ink were the words *This diary is the property of Sarah Chamberlain.*

Em turned to the next page. The paper felt like it was well-made and not likely to crumble on the edges. In the top left corner was a date: June 20, 1860.

Em eagerly read the elegant handwriting.

Oh, what a glorious day! I am sure it could not have been more perfect. My Robert was so dashing in his pearl gray trousers and dress coat. I felt like a princess in a fairy tale in my lavender wedding dress with embroidered pink roses along the bodice and hem. As we stood holding hands before the altar at St. Paul's Episcopal Church saying our vows, I knew my mother must be smiling down on us from heaven.

My infernal hoop notwithstanding, the reception was lovely. It was held on the lawns of the Bolling Estate, with my cousin Beatrice Wainwright as hostess. Robert and I danced and danced, ignoring the talk of unrest between the states being whispered around us. When we tired of dancing, we drank chilled wine and nibbled on exquisite delicacies prepared by the Bolling staff.

I'm too excited to write more, so I will close, dear diary. It is my wedding night after all.

Intrigued with the first entry, Em turned the pages to the last entry. The page was blotchy and some words were too smeared to read. But she could make out enough words to get the idea of what had happened on the last day Sarah wrote in her diary.

June 24, 1865

I have just returned from the funeral. . . . must write . . . while I can think. . . . overcome with despair. . . . need my laudanum and the. . . . of sleep. Amelia and Abby hover . . . concerned.

Robert is dead. . . . blows to the head. . . . three o'clock . . . June 21st. The guard said Robert attacked him. I know . . . account is a lie.

Robert told me last week . . . the Confederate gold. . . . that is why he is dead. . . . murdered my Robert.

I must talk to General Hartsuff. If it's the last thing. . . . I will clear my dear husband's name.

Em closed the diary. *Dead?* Though saddened at the thought of the diary ending with the death of the handsome groom, Em's heart could not help but leap at the thought of the Confederate gold. All her life, Em's parents and teachers had told the story of Jefferson Davis fleeing Richmond with the Confederate gold during the last days of the war. When he was captured in Georgia, he didn't have it on him. In almost 150 years, no one had found the money. Could this diary hold the secret to the location of the missing gold?

A floorboard creaked. Em glanced toward the stairs. She carefully folded the cloth around the diary and placed it back in the hole, then snapped the wooden slat shut. Em stood next to the writing table, trying to look casual.

Her mom appeared at the top of the stairs with a large man grunting from exertion. "Em, this is Mr. Wright of Wright Brothers Antiques. He has offered to replace the missing leg on the writing table for free so we can display it downstairs for our tours of the house by the Petersburg Historical Foundation."

Perspiring profusely in the hot attic, Mr. Wright extracted a large handkerchief from a back pocket and wiped the sweat off his flushed face and neck. He shoved the hankie back in his pocket. Em smiled politely. "That is very generous. Thank you."

Mr. Wright turned to Em's mom, Elisabeth. "Your society has a superb collection of antiques downstairs. The melodeon is an exceptionally fine piece. I would like to examine it, if you wouldn't mind."

"Not at all. During our tours, some of the ladies, including my daughter, dress in period costumes and sing songs from the Civil War era while one of the ladies plays the melodeon."

Mr. Wright examined the writing table. "You were right; this *is* small enough for the two of us to move."

Elisabeth grabbed one end while Mr. Wright bent his portly frame and took the other. Together, they began carrying the table down the attic steps. Em waited in the attic a few minutes, then pressed firmly on the odd looking nail at the edge of the slat. With a click, it opened. Em raised it a couple of inches and removed the bundle. She stared at it. *This diary could hold clues to the gold.* She uncovered the diary and slid it into the front pocket of her baggy capris. After dropping the piece of cloth back in the hole, she closed the secret hiding place.

Once she finished reading the diary, she would give it to her mother. Em stepped to the landing, turned off the light switch, and descended the steps.

During the short drive from the Chamberlain house in Petersburg to her home in Colonial Heights, Em avoided looking at her mother. She often said Em had one of the most expressive faces she had ever seen and that she could never take up a criminal career; she wouldn't be able to lie her way out of trouble.

Elisabeth parked the silver minivan in the driveway of their two-story brick home. As Em got out of the passenger seat, her mother yelled at Caleb, who was mowing the lawn, to hurry and finish. Em's thirteen-year-old brother shook his head and pointed to his ear. Elisabeth pointed to the sky, where dark clouds were building. Em preceded her mom into the house and raced up the carpeted stairs to her room.

"Em, don't forget to finish the laundry," her mother called out.

Groaning, Em headed back down the stairs to the tiny room beside the kitchen. Grabbing fistfuls of damp clothes from the washer, she threw them into the dryer. When she turned the knob and pushed the On button, the machine sprang to life. Em dumped the last load of dirty clothes into the washer, poured in the detergent, slammed the lid, and pulled the knob. She sprinted back to the staircase, taking the steps two at a time and hurrying into her bedroom. Em's mom was a teacher, and now that school was over she was always finding additional chores for Em to do.

After shutting her door, Em reached in her pocket and pulled out the diary. Her body pulsed with excitement at the thought of uncovering a real treasure.

Every July, her extended family rented a house on the beach in Nag's Head, North Carolina. She and Caleb pretended to be pirates. They brought odds and ends from their bedrooms and dug holes in the sand to bury their booty, leaving clues on Post-its around the house.

When she was ten, while digging a hole to hide her brother's baseball, Em had uncovered a gold ring with a small ruby in it. She begged her mom with a hundred "pretty pleases" throughout the rest of the day to let her keep it. With no way to locate the owner, Elisabeth finally agreed. Em put it on the third finger of her right hand, and she hadn't taken it off since.

Em kicked off her sandals and sat on the sage-and-rose-patterned quilt draped across her bed. If this diary held secrets to buried gold, that would make her discovery of a little ruby ring pale in comparison. Leaning against the headboard, Em crossed her legs and opened the dark brown cover. Sliding her finger under the first page, she turned to the second entry.

October 11, 1860

Finally, Robert has located a property of good repute, so this will be our last night at the boarding house. It is located at 515 High Street among other lovely homes and townhouses. I thank our blessed Lord every day for Robert's position as manager of one of the Bollings' tobacco warehouses. The income provides us with quite a decent living. Mama's furniture will arrive at the house tomorrow, the exception being my writing table. A special piece commissioned by my husband, it has stayed here at the boarding house with us.

We have hired two free Negroes, Moses and Rachael, to help with the daily chores. Both of us are in complete agreement that we will own no slaves. Unlike most of our kinsmen, we believe it is a sin to own another human being.

Good night, dear diary. I have a long day tomorrow.

The house at 515 High Street was the one owned by the Petersburg Benevolent Ladies Society. It was called the Chamberlain House after the owner, who donated it to the society. Em turned back to the first page and reread the name: Sarah Chamberlain. This diary must have belonged to the lady who donated the house. And the writing table Sarah mentioned may have been the very one taken from the attic to be restored. A chill traveled up her spine.

Before she could read further, a buzzer sounded. After hiding the diary under her pillow, she jumped from the bed to go switch the clothes from the washer to the dryer and fold the dry ones.

As Em was folding a pair of orange gym shorts, her mother walked into the laundry room. Her amber eyes showed puzzlement.

"Where have you been? I thought we were going to bake chocolate-chip cookies."

"Right. I forgot. Can we do them now?"

Em dropped the shorts into the basket and rushed into the kitchen so her mother wouldn't see her red cheeks. Grabbing two cookie sheets from the cupboard and a roll of chocolate-chip cookie dough out of the fridge, she averted her face until she was sure the flush was gone.

As her mother pulled out the white plastic cutting board, her dad walked into the room. At six foot three inches, he towered over his petite wife. "How are my two favorite girls?"

"Fine, honey." Elisabeth smiled at her husband.

"Good, Dad." Em kept her face averted.

He set his briefcase on the counter as thunder rumbled loudly to the east. Pulling open the kitchen door, Elisabeth yelled for Caleb.

"I'm in the garage!" He shouted back.

Two minutes later, a loud rush of wind accompanied Caleb through the back door. He managed to slam it shut just as the heavens let loose a torrent of rain. Two of the patio chairs blew over and slammed into the deck railing. A deafening clap of thunder followed immediately after a streak of lightning. Em grabbed her dad and held on tight like she was five instead of fifteen. More lightning and thunder followed as the rain pounded the windows. Pulling his daughter close, Daniel wrapped his arms around her.

When the storm passed, and the sky lightened to a dull gray, Em let go of her dad, feeling sheepish over her fear. Giving Em a reassuring wink, Daniel loosened the knot of his tie and left the kitchen to change out of his work clothes. Relieved that the electricity was still on, Elisabeth and Em went back to baking cookies.

Three hours went by before Em could get back to her room. She was chomping at the bit to discover clues about the Confederate gold.

December 21, 1860

Christmas is almost here and I wish I could be more joyful. My home is very festive with all the evergreen holiday decorations. Our Christmas tree came from the Whitakers' farm on the outskirts of the city. Today I strung cranberries and popcorn and wound them among the branches. Next came the bits of ribbon and crocheted ornaments. Last, I clipped candles to a few branches. Robert and I lit the candles together and declared it a masterpiece, and then I burst into tears. Holding me close, he asked what bothered me so. I told him how fearful I was of his leaving me if there was a fight between the states.

After drying my tears with his handkerchief, he kissed me ever so lovingly and told me not to fret so. He said we would carry each other in our hearts if we were separated, and he promised to always return to me.

With a heavy heart, I close, dear diary. I will get down on my knees and pray that the states' differences can be solved without bloodshed.

April 25, 1861

It has happened. This dreadful morn, Fort Sumter was fired on. I am terrified of Robert leaving Petersburg and going to war. I can write no more, for my hand is shaking so badly.

Em sighed. She wasn't interested in the war. But she needed to read every entry so she wouldn't miss any clues to the gold. After flipping the page, she read the next entry.

June 3, 1861

I sit here an empty shell. Robert left today to join President Davis's treasury staff in Richmond. The only blessing in this accursed madness is that he will have a civilian position at the Treasury Department. But he must also join the militia. Although he will not be on the front lines, he could be called up at any time to help defend Richmond.

Neither one of us wishes to give up our home, so we will travel back and forth between Petersburg and Richmond. My sister has a townhouse in Richmond, and I will take the train and stay with her a few days each month.

I am going to miss Robert so much that my heart is already breaking. At the railroad station, I clung to my love, crying my heart out. He wept too, but his tears slid silently down his cheeks.

He is such an honorable man. He does not agree with the politics of the war any more than I do, but he will see *his duty accomplished with integrity. I too must be brave. I am not as optimistic as some who think the war will be won within the year. I must pray to God for strength if I am to make it through these bleak days.*

I will close now, dear diary, as I feel more tears threatening.

Em felt a stirring of sympathy for the couple, mixed with excitement over her first clue. If Robert worked at the treasury until the end of the war, he may have known where the money went when President Davis fled Richmond.

She glanced at the clock on her bedside table. An hour had sped by as she read those few paragraphs. Her eyes were burning, and she knew it was because she was straining to make out the words. Rubbing them, she decided to wait until tomorrow to read more.

Looking around the room, she searched for the best place to hide the diary. She opened her closet door, moved her extra blanket a few inches, and slid the little book into its left-hand corner. As she turned back into the room, her cell phone beeped. Crossing to her dresser, Em picked up the cranberry-colored phone and looked at the screen. Her best friend, Megan, was texting her.

Emily Grace, B-ball 2MRO @ park, 1pm. Tell Caleb.

Pushing buttons, Em texted back.

We'll be there. And don't call me Emily Grace. You know I hate that name.

After snapping her phone shut and setting it on the dresser, Em pulled her long auburn hair out of the elastic band she had twisted it into that morning. Her green eyes were drawn like a magnet to the pale white scar on her neck, from cancer surgery.

Sighing, she pulled her cotton pajamas from her dresser drawer. After changing into them, she went into her bathroom to brush her teeth and comb her hair. Then Em crawled into bed, reached her hand to the lamp switch, and turned it off. Lying on her pillow with her arms crossed beneath her head, she thought about Robert and Sarah. *What did they look like?*

Yawning and suddenly tired, Em turned on her side, cradled her pillow to her cheek, and fell asleep.

Chapter Two

A door slammed, jarring Em awake. She cracked an eyelid and peered at her digital clock. Eight o'clock. She snuggled deeper under the covers.

A few minutes later, a loud knock woke her again. Elisabeth poked her head through the door. "Em, why aren't you up and getting ready for church?

"I'm not going," Em mumbled into her pillow.

"I can't hear you."

Em flopped onto her back and spoke to the ceiling. "I said I'm not going."

"What do you mean? Are you sick?"

Em sighed. "No, Mom. I just don't feel like going."

"But you love church."

Em sat up. "I can miss one Sunday. What's the big deal?"

"Young lady, unless you have a fever, you're going to church." Elisabeth pulled her head back and shut the door. Em tossed off her covers and stomped to the bathroom.

Em's pout lasted about five minutes at the breakfast table before her dad teased a smile out of her. It didn't take much; a wink, a funny face, or a lame joke and her bad mood would disappear.

As Em and her family entered the brown stucco facade of Saint Paul's Episcopal Church on Union Street, the chimes rang. The church had been built in the mid-1800s, and her family had been attending worship services there for generations, since the doors opened for the first time. The Reverend William Pratt, who preached during the Civil War, was an ancestor of Em's on her mother's side.

The ten stained-glass windows that graced the walls of the church shone with colors of the rainbow, depicting various aspects of God's glories. Dark beams and rustic-looking wrought-iron lights passed over Em's head as she walked down the aisle behind her parents. She slipped into a dark wooden pew on the left beside her brother.

Megan and her family came in and sat in the same pew. Megan slid in close to Em. "Guess what?" She whispered.

"What?" Em whispered back.

"I saw Bryan and Leah holding hands at the mall yesterday."

Em snapped out of her mood. "No way! She said boys are only good for two things: basketball and a mean game of Wii."

"Well, I guess she found a third thing." Elisabeth frowned at the girls. Both sat up a little straighter and turned toward the front of the church.

Gazing at the altar, Em thought of Sarah Chamberlain gliding down the center aisle to meet her handsome groom at the altar. In her imagination, Robert was tall and handsome with blond hair, blue eyes, and a full mustache. Sarah had eyes as green as emeralds and coal-black hair curled into ringlets that hung to her waist. Em saw *Gone with the Wind* on DVD last year and imagined Sarah looking just like Scarlett.

The organ started the prelude. Em shifted on the pew cushion and chewed on a hangnail as the choir made their way from the back of the church to the choir loft, followed by the Reverend Marjorie Bevans.

During the hour-long service, Em barely sat still. Her gaze wandered around the church as if she were bored. Megan stared at her twice with a puzzled frown. When church was over, Em could tell Megan wanted to question her about her attitude, but she cut her off by hugging her and saying she would see her at the park later.

At home, Em ate a tuna fish sandwich at the kitchen table. While her family chatted about the trip in July to Nag's Head, her thoughts centered on the last page of the diary. *What was the connection between the gold and Robert's murder?*

"Em?"

Pulled away from her thoughts, Em looked at her mom. "Yes?"

"I'm just wondering what's so interesting in the wallpaper. You've been staring at it for the last ten minutes."

Em said, "I was?"

"You were practically drilling a hole in it with your eyes."

Em shoved the last bite of her sandwich into her mouth. "Guess I was . . . what do you call it?"

"Wool-gathering?"

"Yeah. Wool-gathering." Em glanced at the wall clock. "Oh, man! I have to get to the park by one for a game. Caleb too."

Caleb glanced at Em then finished his apple in two bites and tossed the core overhand into the wastebasket.

"All right. But be home by five."

"Yes, ma'am." Grabbing the apple off her plate, Em jumped out of her chair and raced to her room, where she changed out of her church clothes and into shorts, a T-shirt, and court shoes. Em slipped an elastic hair band onto her wrist, then grabbed her basketball and hand towel out of the chair in the corner of her room. Taking a bite out of her apple, she left her room. Caleb waited for her at the door.

After a ten-minute walk, Em and her brother entered the community park and headed for the basketball courts. Megan was already there, along with five other teenagers. Four were their friends, but the fifth was unfamiliar to Em. Bryan and Leah sat close together on a metal park bench.

Megan smiled at Em and Caleb, and waved them over.

After giving Em a quick hug, Megan turned to the newcomer. "This is Josh Winters. He just moved into my neighborhood a week ago. He'll be a junior this year. I invited him to play today. He's already met Bryan, Tim, Zach, and Leah. Josh, this is Emily Grace Watkins."

Em glared at Megan for using her middle name, then turned to Josh and smiled. "Nice to meet you. Call me Em."

Josh's blue eyes stared at her neck. Self-conscious, Em covered the scar with her fingers.

Josh's face turned pink. "I'm sorry. Very uncool of me to stare. It's just that . . ."

"It looks like someone slit my throat?" Em finished.

"Yeah, kinda."

"Someone did. A doctor. I had a malignant tumor on one of my vocal chords. But the surgeon was able to save my voice."

Josh relaxed as he held out his hand. "In that case, I look forward to pounding you into the pavement if we end up on different sides."

Em's laugh broke the tension as she shook Josh's hand. "You're on."

Josh's handshake was warm and strong. As Em let go, a tingling sensation rushed up her arm.

Feeling flustered, Em turned to her sibling. "This is my brother, Caleb."

Barely listening to their small talk, Em studied Josh. His blond hair was cut short, and wavy bangs covered his forehead. He looked to be about six feet two inches, with a muscular build. *With his good looks, he'd have half the cheerleading squad draped all over him by October.* Em's interest in boys had never been romantic so she was surprised at the twinge of jealousy that accompanied her thought.

Megan called everyone's attention, and Em reluctantly pulled her gaze away from Josh. The five boys and three girls divided into teams, and Em found herself on the opposite team from Josh. Taking a deep breath, she cleared her mind and concentrated on the game.

Megan and Em were the top two girls on their basketball team at school and had no trouble keeping up with the boys. They played off each other well, passing the ball back and forth as they charged to the net. Megan's light brown French braid slapped her back as she went up for a layup, her blond highlights glinting in the sun.

Five minutes into the game, Josh figured out their moves and started guarding Em so Megan couldn't pass the ball. Looking Josh dead in the eye, Em used some of her best fakes to get around him and catch the ball

After an hour, Bryan called a break. Em was dripping with sweat from head to toe and grinning from ear to ear.

Josh wiped his face with a towel. "You're running circles around me, Em."

"Thanks. You had some awesome moves too." Em took a drink from the water fountain. "So, where are you from?"

"Raleigh, North Carolina. My dad changed jobs."

Em rubbed the back of her neck with her towel. "I hope you like it here."

One corner of Josh's mouth curved up. Before he could make a comment, one of the guys called, "Game on!"

Josh pointed a finger at her. "You're goin' down, Watkins."

"Not if I take you out first."

Em played harder than normal that day and her team won. When Josh smacked her palm with his in genuine admiration, Em's heart skipped a beat.

Walking back home with her brother, Em tried to figure out her feelings for Josh. She'd never felt this way about any of the guys she hung out with. They'd always just been friends. Most of them she'd known since kindergarten.

Em wiped her sweaty palms on her shorts. She needed to get a grip on her emotions. She was going to see Josh again tomorrow at the courts, and she didn't want to lose her composure.

Em and Caleb entered the house and bounded up the stairs to their rooms to take showers. After putting on clean clothes, Em wrapped her wet hair in a towel. She reached into the corner of her closet and took out the diary. Glancing at her bedroom door, she debated about whether to lock it. Her mother was sure to become suspicious if she knocked and couldn't get in. She decided against it as she tucked a wet lock of hair up under her towel.

Settling into a comfortable position against the pillows on her bed, Em opened the diary to where she had left off the day before.

August 10, 1861

I have just returned this noon from a five-day visit with my sister, Amelia, in Richmond. The city is bedlam. Volunteers for the Confederate army have poured into the city, and it has grown by threefold. They drill every day and shout in the streets of the swift victory that will be theirs against the North.

I had but a few precious moments each night with Robert. He worked well into the evenings during my visit. His countenance was very serious, and he bid me write down on paper everything he told me so that I might remember. I will do this now.

Because of his proximity in the treasury, Robert constantly hears whisperings among the staff on many aspects of the war. Robert told me he has prayed fervently about what he should look for in the days and weeks to come and he believes God has answered his petitions.

He has said this to no one, but he does not believe the Confederacy will win. He must keep all his opinions to himself, lest someone suspect him of treason. The government plans to hoard all the cotton to drive up the price and put funds in the Confederacy coffers, but Robert believes this will not work. He is a very smart businessman, and his superiors would be wise to take his advice.

He also said the new government will offer bonds for hard currency, and I am to buy none. I am to remove my mother's inheritance in gold coins from the bank and hide it in our house, where only I know the location. I must withdraw all our savings from the bank in gold and silver coins and hide them as well. I am to use the coins *only in a dire emergency. I will continue to use the Confederate money from Robert's pay for everyday expenses as long as they last. Within the next two months, our most precious objects in the house are to be removed and hidden in a location yet to be determined. The war may come to Richmond and the surrounding vicinity, and we must be prepared.*

Oh, dear God in heaven, I am gripped with an almighty fear. Whatever will become of us?

Sarah's anxiety radiated off the page. She understood Sarah's fear to a certain degree; one of Em's cousins was stationed in Iraq. He could be killed by a roadside bomb at any time.

Her eyes drifted back to the entry she just finished. And that's when it hit her. *Sarah hid gold coins in the house!* Maybe she used the hole in the attic. *What if she missed one?* Em decided that she would check the next time she went to the Chamberlain House. She slipped the diary under her pillow to read later that night.

After blow-drying her hair, Em descended the stairs, her fingers trailing on the oak banister. She breathed in the mouthwatering aroma of roast beef and Yorkshire pudding, her favorite meal. A late afternoon sun shone through the bay window in the kitchen, encompassing the room in a mellow light.

"Em, set the table, please." Elisabeth pulled the roast from the oven with her fish-shaped mitts.

"Hon, that roast smells delicious." Daniel gave his wife a kiss on the cheek.

Em laid the last place setting as chairs scraped on the wooden floor. Em's dad said the blessing, and then they all filled their plates.

Caleb sliced through his medium-rare piece of roast. "We met a new guy at the basketball court. His name is Josh. He just moved here from North Carolina."

Having been an all-star on his Virginia Commonwealth University team, Daniel was interested in all things basketball. "Good enough for the Colonial Heights team?"

"Oh, yeah. With him on the team, maybe we can take down Byrd High this year. He pushed Em pretty good."

Shrinking in her seat, Em concentrated on jamming mashed potatoes into her mouth.

"What's your opinion, Em? Is he all-star material?"

Swallowing her potatoes, Em turned to her father. "Too early to tell. I'll let you know at the end of the summer."

Eager to get back to her diary, she finished eating in record time and asked to be excused.

"Going back to your room?" Elisabeth wiped her mouth with her napkin. "Do you have a new book that you just can't put down?"

Why didn't I think of that? Em smiled at her mother. "Yep. It's a story about a writer who goes back in time to the 1700s in Scotland during the war between the Highlanders and the British." It wasn't really a lie; she *was* reading *The Journalist*. It just happened to be on hold until she finished the diary.

"Well, if you can come up for air, we're going to Dairy Queen around six thirty."

Caleb tried to sneak out, but his mom grabbed him by the shirt. "Oh, no, you don't. Your turn to do the dishes, young man."

Laughing at her brother, Em climbed the steps two at a time. She shut her bedroom door and scooted onto the bed. Lifting her pillow, she pulled out the diary and turned to the next entry.

September 26, 1861

I just finished reading all my previous entries and realized I only write in you, diary, during momentous times in my life. I will try to do better and write at least once a month.

The significant occasion this time is the removal of precious items from my house to a safe place I will not mention in this diary. As Moses, Rachael, and I were loading household goods into a rented wagon, Mister Treadmill, my elderly neighbor across the street, gave me a start when he inquired as to whether I was leaving this residence for another. Thinking quickly, I lied more easily than I thought I was capable of. I told him that during the last rainstorm, numerous leaks had appeared in the roof and I wanted to save my most valuable items until repairs could be done. Nodding in approval, he touched two fingers to the brim of his slouch hat and continued with his daily stroll down our street.

Em stopped reading. *I guess I'm not the only one lying for a good cause. If I find the Confederate gold I'll give the reward to my parents.* She looked back at the page.

Robert assures me the Union army will not find the items should the unthinkable happen and the city is overrun. I have seen Robert numerous times since August. Although we won the battle at Manassas, Robert has not changed his mind about the outcome. I trust his judgment.
I am weary from this day's work. Good night, diary.

Em turned to the next entry.

October 20, 1861

A month has passed and, as promised, I am writing in you, diary, before retiring this eve.

I was in Robert's arms a fortnight ago. We spent a splendid week together at my sister's, and my joy knew no bounds. With his strong arms around me, my fear melted away, and I clung to him blissfully throughout those clear autumn nights. Before retiring, we clasped hands and looked at the beautiful stars through the second-story window. Bowing our heads, we thanked our Lord for our time together.

All is quiet, with no fighting for the last few months between the states. One of the reasons for the political unrest is the question of the right to own slaves. I wonder what Moses and Rachael feel about the war, but I will not presume to ask. They are loyal servants who earn the wage I pay them. I am satisfied with both.

I will close now to go to my prayers, dear diary.

Em slipped the diary under the pillow then hopped off the bed to go to Dairy Queen.

An hour later, Em returned, changed into pajamas and picked up reading where she had left off.

November 14, 1861

*I realize that I have not mentioned here the most impor-
tant task I have been involved in since Robert's departure. Twenty ladies, including me, have formed a sewing
circle in the undercroft at Saint Paul's. We have accu-
mulated bundles of rough cloth to make uniforms for
our soldiers. We call ourselves the Petersburg Benevolent
Ladies Society. My task is sewing the buttons on all the
pants and shirts. As long as we have cloth to work with,
we sew every morning and afternoon, except Sunday.
Three ladies in our group are exceptional knitters and
have produced an abundance of socks to keep our beloved
soldiers' feet warm.*

*The hours I work here help me not to fret over Rob-
ert. It is only at night in my lonely bed that fear grips me
and I pray passionately for his safety.*

Adieu for now, dear diary.

Em closed the book and yawned. She crossed the room
and placed the diary on the shelf in her closet. Even with the
break from reading to go to DQ, her eyes still burned. She
wished she could use her Mom's magnifying glass. But what
excuse could she give for wanting it?

As her closet door clicked shut, Elisabeth knocked and
then poked her head into the bedroom. "I'm hitting the hay
early. All the teachers have an end-of-the-school-year meeting
tomorrow morning. Love you. Good night, honey."

Em took a deep breath to still her galloping heart. "Me too.
Night."

Em waited until her mom's door closed, then walked to the spare bedroom where her mom kept the sewing machine and various craft items. She inched out the center drawer of the old pine desk and extracted a round magnifying glass with a black handle. The pea-sized magnifying drop in the right lower corner would be perfect for the words that were most faded. Em slid the drawer closed and tiptoed back to her room.

Chapter Three

For the next two days, Em read three excerpts from the diary in the morning, then rushed off to play basketball after lunch. In the evening, she'd spend a bit of time on the computer or watching television, and then she read another three excerpts before bed. So far her mother hadn't said anything about the magnifying glass.

Em's feelings for Josh turned into a full-on crush. He teased and challenged her on the court, which she hoped meant that he might feel the same. She loved the tingly sensation she got whenever she was around him. She had thought it lame when her friends sighed and giggled whenever cute boys passed them in the hallway at school. If any of her friends found out how she felt about Josh, she was afraid that they would tease her unmercifully.

True to her word, Sarah had written in her diary once a month for the entire year of 1862. Most of her entries covered her daily life in Petersburg and her visits with Robert. As the war progressed, wounded men, many of them quite young, poured into the city from battles raging throughout Virginia. Half of the women from her sewing circle, including Sarah herself, dropped their needles to become volunteer nurses in the makeshift hospitals. Sarah described the unbearable sight of mutilated bodies and missing limbs, and the nauseating smell of infection and unwashed bodies. The most agonizing entry was written in late June. A battle occurred within spitting distance of Richmond, and Sarah didn't know if Robert had gone there to fight. The pages were blurred with Sarah's tears, and Em agonized with her.

As Em reached the midpoint of the diary, she realized she had become emotionally attached to Robert and Sarah. This was no longer just a murder mystery or treasure hunt. Em eagerly devoured each new entry.

One humorous entry in April lightened the overall mood. A stray pig somehow made its way into the house. Sarah, Moses, and Rachael spent a good fifteen minutes trying to corner it. The poor thing squealed its head off as Moses grabbed it and wrestled it out the back door. They butchered it, and the three feasted for a week, sharing some of the meat with Sarah's neighbors.

Woven throughout the excerpts were Sarah's communications with Robert. According to him, the Confederates held their own during the long year of fighting, achieving more victories than the Yankees, but were no closer to winning the war than the year before. Toward the end of 1862, Robert wrote Sarah a letter telling her to start hoarding as many canned and dry goods as she possibly could.

When Em read that Rachael was constantly on the lookout for weevils in the corn meal and flour, she looked up the word. *Yuck! Bugs!*

On Wednesday morning, Em awoke and squinted at the bright sunlight streaming through the window. She'd been so engrossed in her reading the night before, she had forgotten to lower the blinds.

After lunch, she and Caleb went straight to the basketball court. He looked at her with a puzzled frown. "What's up with hiding out in your bedroom lately?"

Trying to appear nonchalant, Em shrugged. "I want to finish the book I'm reading before I start working at the recreation center on Monday."

"And it's taking that long? What is it, a thousand pages?"

"Why do you care?"

Caleb threw his hands up in a backing-off gesture. "Just asking. You normally don't hole up in your room that much."

Grabbing the basketball from his sister, he dribbled down the sidewalk, shifting the orange ball from one hand to the other.

When they arrived at the court, Em was already sweating from the afternoon heat. She used the towel around her neck to wipe off her face. Caleb started practicing layups with Josh. Em stared, her heart pounding.

"Boo!"

Em jumped and glared at Megan, who'd snuck up on her. "Don't do that!"

Her brown eyes twinkling with humor, Megan chuckled. "That was the only way to get your attention. You were in *Josh World*."

"I was not. I was watching Caleb."

"Oh, yeah? Then why is your face turning red?"

Em placed both hands on her cheeks.

"I've known you since kindergarten. You can't hide anything from me."

Em dropped her hands and sighed.

Megan threw an arm around Em's shoulder. "Don't worry. Haven't I always been able to keep a secret?"

Em gave her a hug as Josh and Caleb walked over.

"Your face is all red," Josh said. "Did you jog over here?"

"No, she came here with—"

Em interrupted Caleb. "Yes, I did."

Taking the hint, Caleb kept his mouth shut.

Megan shouted across the court, "All right, you all-star wannabes, let's play some ball!"

At the break, everyone was winded and sweating heavily. Em plopped down on one of the benches and grabbed her towel. Josh sat next to her and glanced at the sun. "I think I'm going to have to call it quits. It's getting too hot."

"Maybe we should switch to mornings." Em said.

"Awesome idea."

Em grinned.

When the rest of the players walked over, Zach suggested they switch to mornings. His red hair had turned brown with sweat and was plastered to his scalp.

Josh and Em looked at each other and laughed. Turning back to Zach, they said, "Excellent idea!"

Everyone agreed to meet at nine the next day. With high-fives all around, the group split up. Smiling at Em, Josh said he would see her in the morning and headed off toward his street with Megan.

Em stopped at the water fountain for a drink. She splashed some of the cool water on her face. Caleb followed suit. They walked home together in companionable silence.

Em climbed the steps to her room. As she reached the top stair, she heard her mom's agitated voice coming from her bedroom. Em paused at the open doorway.

"Katy, please don't cry. We'll figure something out." Elisabeth gripped the phone receiver and wiped tears from her cheeks with a tissue.

Em wondered what was wrong with her aunt. Katy's husband had died of a heart attack two years ago, and she'd struggled financially ever since.

"I know, but you can always live here until you find another place."

Aunt Katy had inherited the antebellum house that had been in Uncle Jackson's family for generations. She loved that house. She and her husband had spent ten years collecting antique furniture for each room.

"Okay, honey. Go lie down and rest. I'll talk to Dan."

Elisabeth turned and jerked back a bit when she saw Em at the door.

"Mom what's wrong with Aunt Katy?"

"Nothing you should be worrying about, sweetie."

Em felt a knot form in her stomach. "Please tell me."

Her mother shifted on the edge of her blue-and-white quilted bedcover and sighed. "She hasn't been able to make mortgage payments for three months. She may have to sell the house. I think we should say a quick prayer." Elisabeth reached for Em's hand.

Em backed away. "My hand's all sweaty. I need to take a shower."

Elisabeth frowned as Em exited her room.

All through supper, Em thought about her aunt. If she could find a clue in Sarah Chamberlain's diary that leads her to wherever the gold was hidden, perhaps she could save her aunt's house.

Before she began to read that night, Em counted the entries she had left. Sarah no longer wrote in the diary every month. Calculating in her head, she figured she could be done by Saturday morning.

With her legs crossed Indian-style on her bed, Em read.

April 29, 1863

It was only four months ago Robert bade me hoard as much food as I was able, and now I learn of the bread riot in Richmond. Food is scarce because of the Union blockade and the need to feed our soldiers. I guess I will be sporting a leaner figure soon.

Moses, Rachael, and I get by. I want to help the refugees who stream into the city, but there are so many of them and not enough food to go around. I gave our cornbread breakfast to a refugee woman with two small children today.

The price for even the simplest food has become outrageous. Molasses is eight dollars a gallon. A dozen eggs cost sixty cents. Meat is seventy-five dollars a pound!

I am weary in mind and body, dear Lord. Please help me stay strong, and keep Robert safe.

As she turned to the next page, Em noticed that the ink was even more faded than the previous pages.

May 25, 1863

The last of my store-bought ink is gone. Rachael now makes ink by soaking the husks of the black walnuts Moses gathered last autumn. Moses has planted a garden from the seeds saved from last year's vegetables. I thank God for the wisdom of my husband. Before Robert left for this godforsaken war, he insisted on putting up a plank fence around the perimeter of the grounds behind the house. No one passing by in the alley can view our garden. Nevertheless, Moses now sleeps outdoors to guard it. He has a large, stout stick. He refuses to shoot anyone over food, and I agree.

Lord be praised, Robert was given a two-day furlough to come home, and we spent a large portion of it, blissfully, in each other's arms. I asked Robert when he thought the war might end, and he just shook his head. He took my hands in his and said I must pray zealously every day. I kissed him tenderly and waved from the porch as he rode back to Richmond on a borrowed horse.

Good night, dear diary.

Em thought about the passages she had just read. *They were practically starving.* Unlike her impersonal history book, the diary entries pulled her in to Sarah's world. She felt Sarah's pain, hunger, fears.

July 23, 1863

I am sorry, diary, for not writing last month, but the day-to-day chores that have to be done just to survive are immense, and I am so weary in the evening I can do no more than lay my head on the pillow and sleep.

Candles have become scarce, so I do not write past sunset anymore. I am writing in you early in the morning because once my day begins, there will barely be time to eat the meager fare Moses and Rachael scrape together: a little bacon (if affordable), peas or another vegetable from the garden, cornbread, and chicory coffee. Flour is too dear. I can no longer afford it.

The battles rage on, and our losses in Pennsylvania and Mississippi were an agonizing blow. Robert believes this is the beginning of the end for the Confederacy. We are losing.

Dear God, what will become of us?

Feeling tears threatening, Em decided she needed to take her mind off of Sarah and Robert. She would log onto the Internet and do some research on the value of gold coins from the Civil War Era.

Walking into the den, Em noticed Caleb sitting on the brown leather recliner in the corner of the room, cleaning one of the three reproduction Enfield rifles that hung above the fireplace. She and her brother were both entered in the rifle firing competition at the Civil War reenactment in Manassas in two weeks. Em had won in her division two years in a row.

Caleb looked up from his task. "Want to place a small wager on who's going to win this year?"

"Okay, Davy Crockett. Can you afford twenty bucks?"

Caleb reached into his pocket and pulled out a twenty-dollar bill.

"You want to throw away your mowing money, you're on." Em walked to the computer and sat down.

After replacing his gun on the hooks over the mantle, Caleb strolled to the desk. "Why are you searching old coins?"

"I'm going to start collecting."

"Give me a break."

Em swiveled the chair toward her brother. "Did I invite you into my business?"

Elisabeth poked her head through the doorway of the den. "Blackberry cobbler is on the table."

Caleb bolted out of the room.

Em looked up at her mom. "How much money does Aunt Katy need to keep the house?"

"I'm not sure, maybe ten thousand dollars."

That was a lot of money. As her mom left the room, Em returned her focus to the computer, wondering how many Confederate coins she'd have to find to make ten thousand dollars.

Chapter Four

After basketball practice, Em opened the fridge, lifted the gallon jug of water off the top shelf, and drank straight from the jug. She shivered with relief as the ice-cold water cooled her overheated body.

"If Mom sees you doing that, you're dead meat."

Em handed the jug to Caleb. "I suppose you plan to use a glass?"

"Heck, no." Caleb grinned and lifted the jug to his mouth.

Em punched her brother in his arm and headed upstairs. After showering and changing clothes, she got the diary and magnifier out of her closet.

September 11, 1863

Robert has been promoted for the second time, this time to captain in the militia. But as I folded my congratulatory letter to him and sealed it with wax, I felt no joy at the news. I fervently want him discharged before he is killed or captured.

Dear diary, do you know what I dreamed of last night? A bowl of peaches simmering in brandy. I never complain about the lack of special treats, but I do miss them. Moses went out foraging yesterday and found a few small pears, peaches, and apples on the trees around Petersburg. They were overly ripe but tasted heavenly to me.

Moses and Rachael have been living in the house with me for the past few months to keep me safe, even though I have had to decrease their wages.

Rachael just came into my bedroom to help me dress, so I will close. Dear Lord in heaven, please relieve this abiding ache in my heart.

As Em closed the diary, there was a knock at her door. She swiftly slid the book under her pillow.

Opening the door a crack, Elisabeth stuck her head in. "Ready for lunch?"

"I'm starving." Em jumped off the bed and lifted the towel off her head. "I'll be down as soon as I comb out my hair."

An hour later, Em was back in her room with the diary on her lap. *Please let there be a clue about the gold so I can help my Aunt Katy.* She turned to the next entry.

December 26, 1863

Robert was allowed leave from the treasury for two days because of the holidays. He left at the break of dawn this morn to return to duty, but oh, how splendid a Christmas it was with Robert home. He brought a present for Christmas, a wild goose. It was a gift from the chef at the executive mansion, who was returning a favor Robert paid him. Although all I had to decorate for the season were a few evergreen sprigs and pinecones, it was still a blessed holiday with Robert holding me by the fireside on Christmas morn.

He had sad news to tell. His best friend from his college days at William and Mary, John Reese, was killed on the battlefield. We bowed our heads and said a prayer for God to welcome John's soul unto His merciful bosom.

I must go, dear diary, for I am off to nurse our wounded, which multiply in number every week. There are no longer supplies, and I have ripped apart my last two spare dresses for bandages. Do you think, dear diary, if the women of Richmond cut up all their dresses and strolled down the streets in naught but their chemises and drawers, that President Davis would finally end the war? It is a thought.

Em laughed out loud at the thought of thousands of women on the streets of Richmond in their underwear.

She turned the page.

February 22, 1864

It is my birthday today, dear diary. I am twenty-two but feel so much older. Rachael baked me a splendid cake made of a little precious flour (from I know not where), sorghum syrup, an egg, and crushed walnuts. I enjoyed it as I looked out the window of my parlor at a foot of glistening snow blanketing our street.

I have been able to visit Robert twice in the last two months, and he has been home once. I mended his coat and darned his socks. Both of us desperately need new clothes, but the material is too dear. I can see the defeat in his eyes as I tenderly hold his face close to mine. All we have to look forward to is more bloodshed when the spring offensives begin.

Oh, Lord, how much more can we endure?

Feeling Sarah's heartache, Em decided to put the diary away and do something to lift her spirits. Her cell phone vibrated on her dresser. Em picked it up, looked at the readout, and pushed the Talk button. "Hey, Megan, what's up?"

"I'm bored. Want to go get some ice cream? My mom has to do some shopping, and she said she'd take us with her to the mall." Megan said.

"Are you reading my mind? I was just about to call you and ask the same thing."

"Great minds think alike. See you in ten."

In the mall's ice cream parlor, Megan and Em reclined in white wrought-iron chairs with backrests in the shape of hearts. Megan's tongue licked around the perimeter of the mint chocolate-chip ice cream in her sugar cone.

"You know, Josh likes you."

"What?" Em's exclamation came out louder than she intended. Three tables of people turned and stared. Unperturbed, Megan continued to eat her treat.

"Are you messing with me?"

"No."

Em stared at her strawberry-cheesecake ice cream cone. "I think you're wrong. There's no way he would ever be into me. Not with this ugly scar."

"It's barely noticeable."

Em gave a weak grin. "You have to say that. You're my best friend."

"And because I'm your best friend, I'm going to tell you to stop with the pity party. I've been watching you guys. It's pretty funny, really. You both look at each other when the other one's not looking."

"Seriously?"

Megan rolled her eyes. "You have got to stop being so obsessed with your scar."

"It's not just that," Em whispered.

"Look, Em, the cancer's not coming back." She squeezed Em's free hand.

Em rubbed the wetness on her lashes with the back of the hand that held her cone.

"Caleb thinks you're hiding something in your room."

Caught off guard, Em was at a loss for words as her ice cream melted in thin rivulets down the side of her cone. She took a huge lick while debating what to say to Megan

"I'll tell you what's going on, but you can't breathe a word."

"Scout's honor. Megan raised the first three fingers of her right hand.

"I found a diary in the attic of the old Chamberlain House. I haven't told my mom because I wanted to read it first. I'm almost finished."

Megan looked at Em. "Your mom is going to ground you for life when she finds out."

A brilliant idea jumped into Em's head. "I have to go with my mom Saturday afternoon to help her and the other ladies clean the house. I'll go up to the attic and pretend I just found it."

"How old is this diary?"

"It was written during the Civil War."

Megan leaned forward. "That sounds pretty cool."

After taking a bite out of her cone, Em lowered her voice. "It's a murder mystery. And the last page mentions the lost Confederate gold." Em got goose bumps just talking about it.

"Why are you whispering?" Megan licked the drips on the side of her cone.

"I'm hoping there's a clue in the diary as to where the gold is hidden."

Megan scoffed. "And you think you can find this lost gold?"

"I don't know. But Sarah talks about hiding gold coins in the Chamberlain house."

"Who's Sarah?"

"She's the one writing the diary. Her husband, Robert, was murdered." Em sighed. "I hate that. They loved each other a lot."

"Can I see the diary?"

"When we get back to my house, you can."

Megan ate the last bite of her cone. "I wouldn't want to have lived back then. I've seen some of the medical instruments they used, in the Siege Museum." She shuddered.

"I don't know," Em said. "It might have been kind of interesting. I don't mean during the war. Maybe after."

Megan's mom walked into the ice cream parlor. "Ready to go to Macy's?"

Em pulled the diary down from the closet and reverently handed it to Megan while her mom waited in the car. Megan turned the cover and read the inscription.

"Sarah Chamberlain. That's the name of the society's house, right?"

"Yes, that's where Sarah lived." Em turned to the last entry. "And this page talks about the murder and the gold."

Megan peered at the page. "I can't make out the words, it's too smeared." She closed the diary and handed it back. "Let me know how it turns out. I've got to go before my mom comes looking for me. Don't forget Bible study at Leah's tonight."

Em stared at the diary in her hand. "I can't go."

"Why not?"

Em racked her brain for a good excuse. "I need to read the rest of the diary for clues."

Megan stared at Em. "That's a lame excuse. And why don't you want to go to Leah's?"

"Your mom's waiting. You better get going."

Megan folded her arms across her ribcage. "Not until you tell me what's going on with you."

"You're not going to want to hear it."

"Try me."

Em sat on the edge of her bed and sighed. "I don't believe the same as I used to about God."

"What do you mean?"

Em's voice rose in anger. "Where was God when I got cancer? Or when my folks lost their savings to pay the doctor bills? Or when our dog, Brandy, got hit by a car and died? And how about my Aunt Katy losing her home?" Tears clouded Em's vision. "Either God doesn't care or he doesn't exist."

Megan stared at her best friend, but didn't say a word.

"Megan, we have to go," A voice shouted from the bottom of the staircase.

"Em, please . . ."

"I'm okay. I'll see you tomorrow."

With a troubled glance at Em, Megan left the room. Em sat on the bed wiping her eyes with the sleeve of her shirt. *Why had she told Megan about the doubts she had been having about God for the last couple of months? She would probably be a prayer request at the Bible study.* Em looked down at the diary in her hand, and her thoughts turned cynical. *Talking to God was a total waste of time.* He didn't care about her or Sarah. Em got off the bed to get the magnifying glass. She crossed to the antique pine rocker with the cane-woven seat and backrest in the corner of her room. She sat down and rocked slowly as she read the next entry.

May 9, 1864

The news from Robert is very bad. Butler's army is closing in on Petersburg and Richmond. We have been lucky so far not to be in the forefront, but our luck appears to have run out. Robert wishes me to leave Petersburg, but where will I go? My father and sister both live in Richmond, and Robert only has one brother, William, who is fighting in Georgia. My cousin Beatrice refuses to leave her home to the mercies of the Yankee savages should Petersburg be taken, and I feel the same.

I fear we are coming to the end, dear diary.

Em closed the diary. "Oh, Sarah," she whispered, "I'm so sorry you lost the love of your life."

Chapter Five

Hearing her parents' voices raised in anger, Em paused at the bottom of the staircase just outside the kitchen. Her dad was usually gone for work by now. *What was going on?*

"What money?" Her father grumbled. "Health insurance only covered eighty percent of the expenses for Em's surgery and treatment. That totally depleted the kids' college fund."

Em gripped the banister. *Great, they were fighting about money again.*

"What if we take out a loan? Katy will pay us back when she can."

"No, Beth. We're not going into debt for that hundred-and-fifty-year-old money pit."

"I know how much you love your sister, but there's nothing we can do."

"You're right." Em heard resignation in her mom's voice. "It's just that she's so devastated."

Taking a deep breath, Em entered the kitchen. "Did your boss give you a day off?" Em asked, hoping to ease the tension.

"I'm the boss, and yes, I did. I can have a day off every once in a while." Daniel picked up the newspaper, the pages rustling as he sought the sports section.

"Something special in the works?" Em teased as she accepted a bowl of oatmeal from her mom.

Caleb entered the room and grabbed a chair at the table. "How about taking us all to Disney World?"

Daniel laughed. "What are you, eight years old?"

"Hey, you're never too old for Disney World." Elisabeth smiled as she handed her husband a glass of orange juice. He briefly squeezed her hand as he took the glass.

"Actually, I took the day off to see if I could help your Aunt Katy. I'm looking into a couple of options."

Em shoveled a spoonful of oatmeal into her mouth. She hoped that whatever the options were, something would work.

Josh waved to Tim as he walked over to the basketball court. He had asked him if they could meet about an hour before everyone else showed up. Tim thought it was to get in some extra practice shots. But Josh wanted to pick his brain about Em. From what he had gathered from the conversations floating around the basketball court all week, besides Megan, Tim seemed to be the closest to Em. Josh wasn't about to talk to Megan. The conversation would get back to Em in two seconds if he knew anything about girls, and he did. His sisters gossiped about boys all the time.

Brushing the blond bangs off his forehead, Josh smiled as he drew closer to his new friend. Tim was about six feet three inches with closely cropped dark hair and coffee-colored skin. He was one of the skinniest guys Josh had ever seen, with big feet and big hands that were perfect for basketball. Tim shot Josh the basketball then high-fived him.

"Hey, man, what's up?"

Bouncing the ball, Josh said, "Not much. You?"

"Just living the good life." Tim grinned. "Ready for a little one-on-one?"

Josh dodged around Tim and went in for a layup. The ball bounced off the backboard and into the goal. Josh tossed the ball to Tim.

While he guarded Tim, Josh said, "Mind if I ask you a couple questions about Em? Just between you and me."

Tim dribbled the ball, looking for the best way around Josh. "Sure."

"Does she have a boyfriend?"

Tim let loose a hoot of laughter. "Em's never liked any boys that way. They're all her buds."

"That's great."

"You thinking of asking her out?" Tim backed up and whooshed the ball at the goal.

"Thinking about it."

"Go for it, man."

Catching the ball from Tim, Josh decided to do just that.

Josh mustered up his courage and approached Em as she was getting a drink at the water fountain during the game break.

"Hey, that last shot of yours was amazing."

"Thanks." Em wiped her mouth with the back of her hand.

Josh twisted the sweat towel with his fingers. "I was wondering if I might call you later tonight."

She smiled. "Sure. Let me give you my cell number."

Josh grinned. "That's okay. I already got it."

"Break's over! Let's play ball!" Tim shouted from the foul line.

They ran back to the center of the court.

Em sat on her bed after lunch, excited with anticipation of Josh's call that evening. *What would she say? She definitely didn't want to say the wrong thing. What if she did say something lame?* Em shook her head. She needed to stop thinking about Josh.

She opened the diary, placed the magnifying glass over the next page, and read.

June 30, 1864

Oh diary, the worst has happened—the war is at our front door, or is it our back door? All I know is that I am desolate and downhearted. Lee's army has come to defend us, and with it, my dear Robert. He has been transferred from the treasury to Company B, 12th Virginia Infantry here in Petersburg.

My heart is full of joy and sorrow at the same time. Although I see him most evenings, I know his life is at utmost risk now. I cowered like a frightened mouse when I first heard the sound of the shells, but Robert assures me our house is far enough up High Street that it most likely will not be hit. If the defenses get moved back, it will be a different story.

I can write no more. I am too low in spirits.

October 14, 1864

I looked at my last entry and could not believe I have not written for four months. Every day is much the same as another. The Union soldiers fire and our men fire back. The constant sound of shells exploding frays my nerves. Grant has gained no ground, but where is the victory?

I fear I am growing cynical. When the women get together, we whisper what most of the men would not like to hear. The South should surrender, to save the lives of the young boys who bravely fight on with no shoes on their feet. Robert knows the cause is lost and wishes, as I do, for terms of surrender. Shaking, I asked Robert what would become of him. He does not know but understands President Lincoln to be a fair man. He believes that he will pardon "the rebels," as the North calls us. May God be merciful and grant that belief.

With a heavy heart, Em laid the diary beside her and decided to take a quick nap before reading more. Two hours later, she turned to the next entry.

December 25, 1864

Today is Christmas, and there is no reason to decorate or celebrate. I have spent most of this day in prayer. I knelt at the pew and begged God's mercy for our fair city. Many of the families who have stayed in town went to the churches with groups of soldiers this morning. Robert and I attended a starvation ball at the Bollings' Mansion two weeks ago. Most of the Bollings family has fled, leaving my cousin Townsend in charge of the mansion.

I am still weak from a fever a few days ago. Rachael brewed a medicinal tea, which has helped quite a bit. I survive each day with nothing but pluck and fortitude.

The guns have slowed as the cold weather has arrived. Robert tells me that with little money and no supplies, the Confederacy will not hold the defenses much longer.

The food is even scarcer than last I wrote. The farmers are afraid to cross the defense lines. About the only meat left to eat are pigeons. Soldiers are deserting daily now to return home and help their starving families. May God have mercy on us all.

Em hid the diary in her closet and headed downstairs to see if dinner was ready. She would try to remember to be grateful everyday that she had plenty to eat. With so few pages left, the odds of finding a clue to the gold were disappearing like snowflakes on warm asphalt.

Em had just finished setting the table when her dad entered through the back door. His face looked strained.

Em steeled herself for bad news. "Any luck?"

Her father ran his hand through his thick hair. "Sorry, Em."

Elisabeth set the big salad bowl in the middle of the light oak table. "Caleb should be in soon with the grilled chicken."

"Yeah, I saw him on the deck, sweating all over the meat."

"That's gross, Dad."

"Just trying to lighten the mood a little. I know we're all upset about Katy losing the house, but it *is* just a house. She has God, her family, and lots of friends."

Em sat at the table as Caleb came through the door with the tray of grilled chicken.

After dinner, Em sat at the computer in the den and tried to Google Robert Chamberlain, but none of the hits pertained to Sarah's husband. Finally giving up, she headed for her room.

As she stepped off the last stair, her mom called out from the kitchen, "Em, don't forget the laundry tomorrow. You need to start a couple of loads before we leave for the Chamberlain House."

Em rolled her eyes. "Yes, ma'am."

After changing into her pajamas, Em pulled the diary and magnifying glass from under her pillow. She curled up on her side and read the next entry.

February 24, 1865

I thought the opposing forces would abide in winter camp until at least March, but because of fair weather at the beginning of this month, a battle was fought by Boydton Plank Road. Robert had to go help defend Lee's position, but thank our good Lord, he has returned to me in one piece.

Grant and his forces did not break through our lines, but oh, how I wish they had. That sounds treasonous, but I want this infernal war to end before Robert is killed.

The four of us are now as thin as rails. Moses is still our miracle provider, going I know not where and finding food to supplement our canning of last summer and fall. I still have a good supply of coins because I did not spend much on the outrageous prices for dry goods and meat. Robert says every penny will be needed when this conflict ends.

He has also warned me several times to keep the rifle loaded because the Yankees soldiers will, no doubt, try to pillage the city before order is restored by the commanders.

I cried in Robert's arms all last eve when he told me to be strong when he becomes a prisoner of war. Neither of us will acknowledge that he could be killed. How can the sun shine so brightly out my window when my heart is so dismal?

Em was about to start the next entry when her cell phone rang. Her heart pounding, Em looked at the screen, then answered with a bright "Hey, Josh."

The two of them chatted for the next hour. All Em's worries were groundless. There wasn't one awkward pause.

Josh asked Em if she would like to go for ice cream the next day.

"Sounds great. But I can't. I have to help my mom at the society's house tomorrow afternoon."

"That's cool. We'll do it another time. See you at the courts in the morning. Bye."

"Bye."

Lowering the phone to the bed, Em worried her lower lip and hoped Josh would ask her again. Not in the mood to finish the diary, Em decided to read the last entries before lunch tomorrow.

Chapter Six

Em opened her blinds to leaden skies and a gentle rain, the kind that was probably going to go on all day. She certainly wouldn't be playing basketball. And that meant she wouldn't see Josh today.

Depressed, she dressed in her baggy beige capris and a white baby-doll top with red trim. It was faded and worn, perfect for cleaning. After grabbing an elastic band off the dresser, she pulled her auburn tresses into a ponytail.

The aroma of waffles cooking didn't raise her spirits as she entered the laundry room to start the first load.

"Em, you ready for some breakfast?" Elisabeth called.

"Be right there." Em loaded dark clothes into the washer, started the machine, and walked into the kitchen.

"What's wrong, baby? You look like you lost your best friend."

Em pulled at her fingers. "Do you remember that new guy, Josh, that we talked about at dinner the other night? Well, I kind of like him. But don't tell Dad or Caleb. Promise?"

"I promise." Elisabeth put a plate of waffles and bacon in front of her daughter. "But this is world-shattering news." She winked.

Em reached for the syrup on the table. "He wanted me to go for ice cream this afternoon, but I told him I couldn't 'cause I have to go to the society house." She poured syrup on her waffles, hoping her mom would offer to let her out of the cleaning project.

"I'm sorry, Em. But Angie cancelled, so it's just you, me, and Jill to clean that whole house before the next meeting."

Snapping the cap back on the syrup, Em sighed. "Where's Caleb?"

"I assume he decided to sleep in when he saw the rain." Elisabeth sat at the table and took a bite of her bacon. "So, tell me about this boy."

"Well, he's really cute. He has blond hair. And he's a great b-ball player." She chewed on a forkful of waffle. "You'd like him. He's respectful. And he doesn't seem to care about my scar."

"Honey, the scar only bothers you. I don't even notice it anymore. I knew once you became interested in boys, you'd be a good judge of character. I'm glad you shared this little secret with me. Care to share the other one?"

Em stared at her plate. "I don't know what you mean."

"I think you do."

Em looked up at her mom. "There is something, but I need to think about sharing it. Can you give me a little more time?"

Her mom poured syrup on her waffles. "Deal."

After switching the loads of laundry, Em went back to her room. She felt bad now about not telling her mom about the diary right away. She would finish it and then give it to her.

Em took the diary off the closet shelf, along with the magnifying glass, walked to the rocking chair, and settled in.

April 7, 1865

Oh, diary, the inevitable has finally happened. Five days later, I still shake as I write this passage. Petersburg, our fair city, has fallen and surrendered. It happened on April 2nd. On the evening of April 1st, Robert raced into the house, shouting my name. He informed me that Lee was evacuating the city, and he was ordered back to Richmond. I clung to him desperately and begged him not to go. He clasped my hands, kissed me gently, and told me confidently that we would be together again and that God would watch over us both. I took the lace handkerchief out of the pocket of my skirt and gave it to Robert. He took a deep breath of the perfume clinging to it and shoved it inside his coat. With tears streaming down my face, I stood in staid silence as he rode off on his horse.

The next day was utter chaos. Three Union soldiers knocked on the door and informed me they were to search the house for hidden rebels. They are doing this at all the homes. I quaked in terror, but they turned out to be quite polite and said to inform the occupation garrison if there was any unruly behavior or invasion of our home by Union soldiers.

The next eve, an inebriated soldier did try to break in the house, but Moses chased him off with his stout stick.

I have not heard from Robert and am very worried. The rumors fly as to which sections of Richmond have been shelled and torched. If I don't hear from him soon, I know I will go crazy.

So Robert went back to Richmond to be with President Davis. Excited, she thought that if he was with Davis, he was also with the gold!

Em was eager to read the next entry, but she had another load of clothes to put into the dryer. She raced downstairs, threw them in, and hurried back to her room.

April 17, 1865

I am in shock over the most horrible news. President Lincoln has been assassinated! What will happen to Robert, to us all?

A gentleman friend of Robert's has sent word that Robert was to accompany the treasury funds from Richmond with Jefferson Davis and members of his staff. He has no information on where they have gone. General Lee has surrendered, and the war is all but over.

My niece Abby has come from Richmond to keep me company during this trying time. She is such a blessing. Please, Lord, keep my Robert safe.

Em bounced up and down on the bed. *Robert did travel with the gold.*

June 2, 1865

Oh, what splendid news! Robert, who was captured with President Davis and other gentlemen on May 10th, has been sent to the temporary prison here in Petersburg to await parole for his "treasonous" deeds against the United

States of America. On May 29th, President Johnson issued a proclamation of amnesty and pardon for the Confederate states.

I was able to visit with Robert yesterday and rejoice over the wonderful news. As soon as the paperwork is ready, Robert will swear an oath of allegiance and come home. I have used a few of the precious coins to purchase supplies from the sutler at the garrison. The food rations given out at the military commissary are quite edible. I try not to be depressed about what the future holds for us, leaving it in the hands of our almighty God.

June 18, 1865

Oh, diary, I am so very grateful. I found out a few days ago that Robert is to be pardoned on June 22nd. I cannot wait.

I must mention a conversation Robert repeated to me today. The two soldiers who guard him said they believe Robert knows where the Confederate gold is because he traveled with Davis when he left Richmond. He informed them that it was not his business to know the whereabouts of the monies of the Confederacy, and they would have to direct their questions to the secretary of the treasury. Robert told me they were a couple of dimwitted louts and did not understand his wit. Angry, one of them roughed him up a bit in the small office at the tobacco factory, where he is being held.

I was concerned for his well-being, but he said he was fine and not to have a timid heart. The guards were just trying to frighten him into giving up information he doesn't possess. He was more concerned for my safety. He told me that to err on the side of caution, I should apprise Moses of the situation so he could keep a watchful eye.

Only a few more days, dear diary!

Em stared at the page she had just finished reading. There was only one entry left and she already knew what it said. Robert never told Sarah anything about the Confederate gold because he didn't know the final location. Or maybe he was protecting Sarah.

Poor Aunt Katy. She would never be able to help her keep her house now.

Before reading the last entry again, Em turned back to the page that mentioned the coins Sarah had spent at the sutlers. Some of the gold coins Em had researched on the Internet were worth thousands of dollars.

Em wondered if there was any chance gold coins might have been put into the secret hiding place in the attic. *And what if one had been left in there by mistake.* It was a long shot. But hope lifted Em's spirits as she picked up the magnifying glass and reread the last entry.

June 24, 1865

I have just returned from the funeral. . . . must write . . . while I can think. . . . overcome with despair. . . . need my laudanum and the . . . of sleep. Amelia and Abby hover . . . concerned.

Robert is dead. . . . blows to the head. . . . three o'clock . . . June 21ˢᵗ. The guard said Robert attacked him. I know . . . account is a lie.

Robert told me last week . . . the Confederate gold. . . . that is why he is dead. . . . murdered my Robert.

I must talk to . . . General Hartsuff. If it's the last thing . . . I will clear my dear husband's name.

Em now knew why there were brown splotches on this page. They were Sarah's tears for her dead husband. He survived through the whole war only to be murdered by a greedy guard.

Tears ran down Em's cheeks as she closed the diary and rose from the rocker. She set the diary on her nightstand and pulled a tissue from the box next to her lamp. After wiping her misty eyes and runny nose, Em stared out the window at the rain splashing into the puddles on the driveway. She wondered if Robert's name had ever been cleared.

"Em, honey," Elisabeth shouted from the bottom of the stairs. "We need to eat lunch so we can get over to the house."

Em turned toward the door. "Give me a few minutes." She went into the bathroom and splashed cold water on her face. She took a couple of deep breaths and reached for the towel on the rack. Em returned to the bedroom, slipped on her shoes and then headed downstairs.

After eating turkey pita wraps and oranges, Elisabeth and Em walked through the back door to the garage.

"Oh, Mom, hold on. I'll be right back."

Em ran through the kitchen and up the stairs to her room. She picked up the little leather diary from the nightstand and put it in the right pocket of her capris.

When her mother stopped the van beside the concrete curb in front of the Chamberlain House, Em looked at it for the first time as Sarah's home. Built in the 1850s, it was a simple and unadorned brick house with three chimneys, two on the left and one on the right. Cracks in the brick ran down the left upper corner and under two windows on either side of the front door. The quiet street was inhabited by neighbors middle-aged and above. A small dormer window stared blankly from under the sloped roof of the attic.

The rain had lightened to a drizzle as Em hurried up the short concrete walkway to the porch. She glanced at the basement windows. In Sarah's time, the kitchen was in the basement, and that is where Rachael would have cooked all the meals. She climbed the steps to the front door. To the left of the doorframe hung a bronze plaque that read.

THE CHAMBERLAIN HOUSE
Donated by Sarah Chamberlain to the
Petersburg Ladies Benevolent Society

Em's mom unlocked the door, and the two of them entered the stuffy house. "I'd like you to dust the parlor and dining room first. I need to get the box fan out of the attic so we don't have to turn on the air."

"I'll get it for you." *This would be the perfect opportunity to check the hiding place for coins.*

"Thanks, honey."

Climbing the steps two at a time, Em quickly reached the attic. She walked over to the hinged plank. Dropping to her knees she pressed the nail and lifted the slat. After it opened, she reached in and pulled out the cloth the diary had been wrapped in. Sliding her arm back into the hole, she felt all around, but nothing except the wood of the enclosure touched her fingertips. The hiding place was empty.

Em sighed and dropped the cloth back in the hole. Because her thoughts were consumed with the possibility of finding a gold coin, she forgot her plan to return the diary to the hole and then tell her mother that she had just now discovered it.

After returning the plank to its place, she stood and scanned the floor for more hiding places. Em walked over the exposed floor of the cluttered attic. There were no other nails like the one over the hiding place.

"Em, what's taking so long?"

"Sorry, Mom," Em yelled down the stairs.

She grabbed the fan and hauled it down to the second-story bedroom where her mom was vacuuming. Em plugged it in, turned it on and descended the stairs to the first floor.

Em walked across the faded Persian runner in the hallway to the door to the kitchen. The back parlor had been converted into a kitchen sometime in the twentieth century and was a mishmash of changes from different decades. The fireplace had been bricked over. A porcelain sink was installed in the 1940s. The antiquated faucets had been replaced with shiny chrome. The refrigerator was twenty years old, and the stove was even older. Cracked and discolored, the linoleum needed to be replaced. Everything looked ancient to Em's eyes. Yet Sarah would have found it all quite modern.

Em pulled a dust cloth and revitalizing oil out of the cabinet under the sink. After working a good amount of oil into the cloth, Em left the kitchen.

As she headed toward the living room, the front door opened, and Jill Thompson breezed in with a cheery "Hello!"

A brightly colored macramé headband encircled her head of curly gray hair. Her skinny frame was draped with a loose white blouse and flowing, red skirt that touched the tops of her leather sandals when she moved. Granny glasses completed the image of a hippy from the 1960's; Em had seen in a picture somewhere.

After answering Jill's greeting, Em pointed upstairs. Jill gave a backhanded wave as she climbed the stairs.

Em paused at the threshold of the front parlor. Above the fireplace hung a portrait of the Chamberlain family. She wondered if one of the females could be Sarah. She'd had no interest in the portrait until today. Two gold satin-tufted chairs, three small mahogany tables with marble tops, and the rosewood melodeon were the only original pieces of furniture in the room.

Em didn't know enough about life in the mid-nineteenth century to imagine what the room might have looked like.

She carefully ran her cloth over every wooden surface, then crossed the hallway to the dining room. The only original piece here was the sculptured walnut china cupboard in the corner.

As Em dusted the dining room table, her mind buzzed with questions. What had happened to Sarah? Where would Aunt Katy live? Would Josh ask her out again? She found herself rubbing the oil into the surface harder than she should. After she finished polishing the cupboard, she turned to the stairs.

"Mom, I'm done," she called up the steps. "What's next?"

"The scuff marks on the kitchen floor."

Em groaned at the thought of scrubbing that nasty floor. Returning to the kitchen, Em opened the cabinet under the sink and yanked out a new rag and citrus oil. "Guaranteed to get rid of scuff marks," the label proclaimed. Squirting the orange oil directly on a scuffmark, Em took the rag and started to scrub. Within seconds, the black mark was gone.

As Em scrubbed the floor, the emotions she'd tried to keep bottled up the last few weeks spilled out. "God, why don't You care about the people who need You? Why did You let me get cancer and let my dog die? My Aunt Katy's faith is awesome, but You haven't even helped her!"

The more she talked, the more frustrated she became.

"And what about Robert and Sarah? They prayed and devoted their lives to You through that whole stupid war. And you let that guard murder him!"

"Em, what's all that yelling about?"

Em winced and shouted the first lame excuse that came to mind. "Uh, I just saw some cockroaches."

"Well, stomp on them instead of yelling them to death!"

Em laughed. But as she squirted oil onto the next black mark, her anger returned. "You know what, God? This is our last conversation, because I've decided You don't exist."

As Em scrubbed her vision wavered and then doubled. She dropped the rag and shut her eyes. When she opened them, the room started spinning. Em threw both hands onto the floor to make the spinning stop, but it didn't help. Breathing hard, she felt certain she was going to throw up any minute. Her hands slid out in front of her, and she collapsed onto the slick linoleum.

Well, if I'm sick, at least I won't have to clean any more scuffmarks, she thought just before she passed out.

Chapter Seven

Em struggled her way back to consciousness. Moving her cheek on the floor, she puzzled at the sensation. Linoleum was supposed to be smooth and hard, not soft. She slowly opened her eyes. She lifted her head and tried to focus. She saw a table leg about a half of an inch from her nose. Scooting on her belly a couple of inches away from the table leg, Em prepared to push herself up to a sitting position. Her eyes widened. Her hands were on either side of a large, red rose embroidered into a rug. She jerked in shock, banging her head on the bottom of a wooden table.

"Ouch." Em rubbed the top of her head.

After scooting backward so she wouldn't hit her head again, Em sat up and looked around the room. Gone were the sink and the shiny, new chrome faucets. And the refrigerator and stove. In fact, the whole kitchen had disappeared, along with the worn linoleum. *That's no great loss; in fact, that's the best part of this crazy dream I'm having,"* Em thought.

Em's brows knitted together. She must be dreaming, although she couldn't remember ever having the sense of touch in a dream. Her fingers rubbed across the pile of the rug.

On the ledge over the fireplace, which was no longer bricked in, sat a clock. It ticked rhythmically and showed the time to be ten o'clock. To the right of the fireplace was a needlepoint chair. Two dark-wood chairs faced each other, their cushions upholstered in a floral pattern. One rested to the left of the fireplace, the other was next to the doorway. Each chair had a walnut wooden table next to it, with an oil lamp on each. Against the far wall was a settee, the cushion a slightly worn dusty rose. The walls were painted a moss green. The heavy drapes on the windows matched the settee. Chills ran down Em's spine. *It all looked so real.*

Turning around to look behind her, Em saw the antique writing table that had been sent out to be restored. A wooden chair perched between the side drawers.

Trembling, Em pushed herself up on shaky legs. She tentatively touched the smooth surface of the writing table.

"Mom!" Em screamed.

A door slammed, and Em heard footsteps.

But instead of her mother, the biggest black man Em had ever seen filled the doorway. He wore a stained and faded white shirt and calf-length brown work pants. His feet were bare and covered in dirt. His short-cropped hair looked like a gray Brillo pad. He brandished a long-handled, curved knife.

Em took a step backward, lost her balance, and fell, hitting her head on the mantle of the fireplace. Pain exploded in her head. She crumpled to the floor.

The large man's surprise at seeing a stranger in the house changed to concern when he saw the young white woman collapse. He dropped the sickle and rushed to her.

Two pairs of rushing footsteps came down the stairs into the hallway. The man turned at the gasps that emitted from the women.

"She done tripped an' fell, Missus Sarah, an' hit her head on da mantle."

"Lord in heaven." Sarah rushed to the man's side. "Go to the root cellar and chip a piece of ice off the block, and bring it here in a clean rag."

As the man ran off to do her bidding, the young woman in the doorway asked, "Is there anything I can do, Aunt Sarah?"

"Yes, Abby. Bring me the pillow off the settee."

Lifting her skirts, Abby rushed over to the settee and grabbed the small needlepoint pillow. With her skirts in one hand and the pillow in the other, she skirted around the card table with the green felt top and handed the pillow to her aunt. Sarah gently lifted Em's head and placed the pillow beneath it. Tenderly, she smoothed stray tendrils of auburn hair from Em's pale face.

"Who are . . . ?"

Before she could finish her sentence, the large man arrived with the ice wrapped in a clean cloth. He handed her the cold bundle. Sarah placed the ice beneath the girl's head.

The back door opened and shut.

"Rachael," Sarah called out, "I have need of you quickly."

A petite colored woman with a woven basket clutched in her hands appeared in the doorway.

Dropping the basket, Rachael hurried to her mistress's side. "Land sakes, Missus Sarah, was wrong wit dat child?"

"She must have bumped her head on the mantle and fainted. Moses found her."

Moses nodded. "She sho' hit her head mighty hard."

Rachael lifted Em's head and examined it with her strong brown fingers. "She done got a bump 'bout da size of a hen's egg."

"Would it be all right to move her?" Sarah asked.

"Sho'. Moses can carry her up da stairs an' put her on Miz Abby's bed."

Moses picked up the girl easily. With Rachael holding the compress to the back of her head, the four of them made their way up the flight of stairs to the second floor. The first door on the right led into the room Abby was occupying during her visit with her Aunt Sarah. Moses laid the stranger on the cream-colored quilt covering the bed. Rachael adjusted her head on the pillow with the compress underneath.

"Moses," Sarah said, "do you know anything about this young woman?"

"No, Missus Sarah. I hear'd someone yell, an' I come a-runnin'. I seen her standin' in da parlor. Den her eyes got big like an she tripped."

Sarah frowned as she tried to remember if the front door had been locked. "So you didn't see her enter the house?"

"No, ma'am."

Sarah turned to Rachael and Abby. "Do either of you recognize this young lady?"

"No, ma'am," both replied.

Abby rubbed her hands together. "Why do you think she was in your house in only her undergarments?"

"That is a very good question."

"I hear'd talk while I was at da market dis morn," Rachael said. "Two white women said a young girl was attacked roundabout here by some no-good Yankee, an' she done left her house screamin'."

Moses, uncomfortable with the young girl's state of undress, cleared his throat and asked if he could go back to cutting down weeds in the garden. Sarah nodded and Moses left the room.

Sarah let her eyes roam over the girl's clothing from head to toe. She appeared to be wearing a loose-fitting chemise with red embroidery. Her drawers were made of heavy cotton. On her feet were brown slippers of a style she had never seen.

Sarah gazed at the girl with furrowed brows. "We'll just have to wait for her to regain consciousness to get our questions answered."

"Rachael," Sarah said, "could you stay and watch over her until she awakens?"

"Yes, ma'am." Rachael pulled the walnut rocker from the corner of the bedroom closer to the bed.

The faded skirts of Sarah's blue, yellow, and brown plaid dress whooshed as she left the room with Abby close on her heels. She passed the staircase and entered her room on the left. Sarah sat down at the sewing machine to continue altering the dress on which she had started earlier that morning. Abby picked up the lace collar she had thrown onto the seat of the rocking chair when she had jumped up earlier to follow her aunt downstairs. She picked up the needle and thread attached to the collar and tried to concentrate on repairing the rip in the lace. Not wanting to disturb her aunt's thoughts, she kept her uncertainties to herself as she plied her needle.

Slowly regaining consciousness for the second time in as many hours, Em's eyes fluttered open, and she emitted a low groan. Rachael awoke at the sound and leaned forward in the rocker. As Em focused on her surroundings, a face came into view. The skin was nut brown and unblemished. Brown eyes with golden flecks and small crinkles in the corners stared down at her, and the generous mouth smiled.

"'Bout time you woke up," the woman said cheerily.

Em felt puzzled but not frightened. "Who are you?"

"I's called Rachael. I works fo' Missus Sarah."

Em turned her head to look around the room, but that small movement caused pain to shoot through her skull. She groaned again. Rachael rose up out of her chair and placed her hand gently on Em's forehead.

"Now, you lay still. You gots a nasty bump on da back of yo' head."

"What happened to me?" Em heard her voice quaver.

"You hit yo' head on da fireplace mantle. Knocked you clean out."

Rachael rubbed Em's forehead with soothing fingers. "Now, jus' lay quiet-like while I go git Missus Sarah."

After Rachael left, Em tried to look around her without moving her head. She was lying on a four-poster bed with a beige canopy above her. A washstand stood in a corner with a cream-colored bowl and pitcher on it. Next to it was a plain wooden chair with a hole in the seat and a pot beneath it. Nothing looked familiar. Hearing voices, she shifted her eyes toward the door as two strange women entered.

The women walked to Em's side. The older-looking one had hair the color of honey, pulled back in a snood. The younger had a luxurious mane of dark brown hair, flowing in ringlets almost to her waist.

"How are you feeling, Miss?" asked the blonde woman, concern evident in her vivid blue eyes. "My name is Sarah Chamberlain and this is my niece, Abby."

Em thought Sarah's name sounded vaguely familiar. But then her head started to pound, and the thought evaporated.

"My head hurts. A lot."

"I am not at all surprised. You took a terrible spill." Sarah lightly touched Em's hand, lying limply on the coverlet. "Can you tell me who you are?"

"I'm . . ." Em stopped. What was her name? She should know that, shouldn't she? Concentrating made her head hurt more, but she got the faintest glimmer of a name, or at least part of one. "Em?"

The younger woman peered at her. "Do you mean Emily?"

The glimmer grew brighter. "Yes. Emily Grace."

"What is your last name, dear?" The older woman squeezed Em's hand.

No matter how much she concentrated, no name came to her. Tears pooled in her eyes. "I don't know."

"It's okay, dear. Bumps on the head can cause you to forget things. Abby and I will let you rest some more. Rachael will bring you up some willow-bark tea for the pain."

As they smiled at her, Em studied the two women, hoping for a spark of memory. Both women were quite beautiful. Em sighed. She didn't recognize either one.

Sarah turned to Rachael and whispered. "After she partakes of the tea, have her slip under the covers for a good, uninterrupted slumber. There are to be no more questions until she has rested."

"Yes, ma'am." Rachael left the room.

"We'll return in a little while, Emily Grace."

Em closed her eyes as Abby and her aunt left the room.

Sarah entered the front parlor and gazed out the window. Abby lifted the skirts of her mauve dress with thin, black stripes and settled herself on the cushion of the gold satin-tufted sofa.

Sarah turned to Abby. "Let's say a quick prayer for Emily Grace."

Sarah sat beside Abby. The women clasped hands and bowed their heads. "Dearest Father in heaven," Sarah murmured, "help this frightened young woman remember her identity so she may return to the bosom of her family. Amen."

They raised their heads just as Rachael's footsteps echoed on the stairs.

"You jus' give me two minutes, Missus Sarah, an' yo' supper will be on da table."

"No hurry, Rachael. Abby and I will enjoy the sun and gentle breeze coming through the window. "

Sarah and Abby sat at the dining room table. Made of walnut, it had a natural luster rather than the shine of polishing oils, which were still too dear to purchase. As Rachael hovered in the background, ready to serve the meal, Sarah picked up the linen napkin with her mother's initials engraved in the corner.

Fingering the embroidered letters, Sarah sighed. "I wonder what mother would have done in this situation. I'm afraid I feel a bit out of my element."

Abby touched her aunt's fingers. "Exactly as you have done. She would have been proud of you." She squeezed her aunt's hand. "You are the strongest person I know. Look at all the horrors you endured during the war and you have come through unscathed. Your dear Robert languishes in that awful prison, and you go every day to lift his spirits and make him laugh. Emily Grace is a lucky young lady to have fallen into your hands."

Boosted by Abby's confidence in her, Sarah smiled and turned to Rachael.

"Rachael, please go ahead and finish your chores. We will serve ourselves."

"Yes, Missus Sarah."

As Rachael left, She picked up the plate of bacon and passed it to Abby. Using a set of tongs, Abby placed two slices on each of their plates. They added tomato slices and cornbread to their meal. Once the food was distributed, Sarah bowed her head and thanked the Lord for providing the meal.

After the women said amen, Abby placed her napkin in her lap. Picking up her knife and fork, she gingerly cut the tomato slice on her plate. She placed a small piece in her mouth, and chewed slowly, savoring the taste. "This is delicious."

"The tomato vines have thrived this year. I believe they are as relieved as we are that the war is over."

A few minutes passed as Abby and Sarah enjoyed their simple fare. Last year, meat was almost impossible to come by, and cornmeal had been scarce. Most families had survived on canned goods, vegetables from their gardens, and a little molasses and cornmeal. Sarah had a bit more variety because Moses was a great forager. Sometimes he would find wild game, an opossum, or a duck. A few times, he had even captured a stray chicken in the woods, let loose by a farmer who was fleeing the encroaching Union army.

Abby took a sip of water. "I received a letter from my mama and papa yesterday. They will be coming from Richmond to collect me Saturday if that is satisfactory with you. They believe once Uncle Robert is released, you'll need time to yourselves."

Sarah's hand caressed Abby's cheek. "You have no idea what a blessing you have been for me these last two months. I was sick with worry when Robert left with President Davis. Your coming to stay with me has helped keep my mind from straying to the worst possible scenarios."

"Papa tells me that most of the wounded soldiers in his hospital have gone home to their families. Only the most grievously injured remain. He will be glad to have me back at the hospital to help nurse the patients that are still recovering."

Sarah swallowed a piece of her cornbread. "What of your young man? Won't he miss you terribly when you return home?"

Blushing to the roots of her dark mane, Abby ducked her head. "He isn't *my* young man."

"He appeared most ardent when he came to tea yesterday. I believe that was his fourth visit in two weeks."

"Do you really think so?"

"Oh, he is definitely quite smitten. If you play your cards right, you could be married by next week."

Abby giggled behind her hand. "Lieutenant Hackett does not wish to be betrothed anytime soon. We are merely enjoying each other's company. He does not mind that I have a brain in my head. We have heated arguments about our politicians in Washington. He applauds me for the passionate things I believe in."

"Sounds quite a bit like Robert."

Glancing at the wall clock, Sarah pushed her chair from the table. "Look at the time; I must be off to visit Robert. Would you keep an eye on Emily Grace?"

"Of course." Abby dabbed at her mouth with her napkin.

Rachael appeared to clear away the dishes.

Chapter Eight

Sarah plucked her brown silk bonnet from the ornate hallstand by the door, settled it on her head, and looked in the mirror as she tied the long ribbons beneath her chin. She draped the fringed shawl around her shoulders and flexed her fingers as she drew on her linen gloves. Sarah swept her skirts through the front door, then shut and locked it behind her.

When Moses emerged from the shadow of the house, Sarah laid her hand over her heart in surprise. "Land's sake, Moses, you gave me a fright!"

"Sorry, Missus Sarah. I's jus' waitin' to take you to Mista Robert."

"There is no need. The prison is only three blocks."

Moses shook his head. "I promised da Mista I'd watch over you. He'd have my hide iffen I let you go by yo'self."

Sarah sighed as she stepped off the porch. "Very well. Thank you."

Sweating slightly beneath the snood at the back of her neck, Sarah walked beside Moses to the McCulloch Tobacco

Factory on the corner of High and Lafayette Streets, which had been converted to a temporary prison for soldiers of the confederacy.

Moses knocked on the wooden door of the rectangular brick building. A key turned, and the door was opened by one of the guards, Corporal Hinkle. Although short in stature, the body inside the federal uniform was solid muscle from years of working on the docks of New York City. His beady eyes traveled hungrily over Sarah's body as she crossed the threshold. Moses glared at the guard.

"Don't you eyeball me, slave boy." The corporal growled as he slammed the door in Moses's face.

"You have no right to be rude to my servant. I shall have a word with your superiors."

Hinkle opened his mouth to retort, but apparently thought better of it. He needed her husband in a good mood when she left.

Sarah saw that Robert was taking a nap in the huge room. It held no cells. There had been only a few officers assigned to this building, while the prisoners awaited their pardons. The room was empty save for a few abandoned tobacco presses, which looked like iron boxes with large wooden screws in them. She called Robert's name. He stirred at the sound of her voice.

Brushing past Hinkle, Sarah hurried across the wooden floor to Robert's cot against the far wall. He rose, and they hugged each other fiercely.

"Oh, darling," she asked, "how are you?"

He pulled away and smiling, Robert said, "Always better once you arrive."

Sarah smoothed Robert's raven locks, which fell almost to his shoulders, and touched his frayed linen collar, dirty with grime. "I wish I had a clean shirt for you."

"No matter, my love. The war is over, and we'll soon get new clothing."

Sarah removed the brown bonnet and gloves and set them on a corner of the cot. She arranged her skirts as she sat on a plain wooden chair beside the cot. "I have two pieces of news. First, Colonel Jacobs stopped by our house yesterday evening." His wife passed away last month while giving birth to his son—a terrible tragedy. "At any rate, he brought a trunk full of his wife's clothes, which he insisted I accept."

"The poor man probably could not abide looking at them any longer."

"I am altering one now so that I may finally change from this dress I have worn for the past year and a half."

Robert picked up Sarah's hand. "You would look beautiful in anything." "And the second bit of news?"

"Oh, Robert, the oddest thing happened this morning. A strange girl appeared in our parlor, tripped, hit her head on the fireplace mantle, and fainted. Moses carried her upstairs, and we put her on Abby's bed. When she awoke, she had no memory of who she is."

"That is very puzzling. What do you plan to do about her?"

"Keep her with us for now and hope she regains her memory."

"Are you sure that is wise?"

Sarah smiled. "She is about Abby's age and quite weak. I don't imagine she will throttle us in the middle of the night."

Robert gazed at his wife. "Pluck and fortitude are your middle names. I trust your judgment, sweetheart."

Sarah looked around the room for the only other prisoner, but noticed no one except the two guards in the manager's office. "Where is Lieutenant Sutherland?"

"He was pardoned today."

Sarah clapped her hands together. "How marvelous!" "It is a shame we still have to wait until Thursday for your pardon. I am pining for your presence at home."

Robert rested his forehead against Sarah's. "As am I, my love."

Sergeant Bowers sat behind a desk in the manager's office, staring at the lovebirds. His Springfield rifle lay across his lap. Hinkle sat on the other side of the desk picking his teeth with a sliver of wood. He turned to Bowers and pursed his lips. "Now don't play hard to get. How's about a little kiss for your sweetheart?"

"Unless you want a broken nose to match mine, you'd better shut your trap."

In no mood to banter, Bowers stared at Robert and Sarah. Drafted from the docks along with Hinkle, he had been forced to march south with the Union Army. The lousy food, abysmal weather, and constantly being shot at had further soured his disposition. Someone owed him big for the inconveniences of his life, and that someone was Captain Chamberlain.

He had heard rumors that Chamberlain knew where the Confederate gold was because he had been on the train with the gold as it left Richmond. If Chamberlain thought he could keep all that gold to himself, he had another thing coming.

Bowers and Hinkle had been planning for the last week about how to bring up the subject of the gold to the captain. Chamberlain was the only prisoner still incarcerated. There would be no other prying eyes as they approached him. Bower reached into the worn leather pouch in his lap and put another plug of tobacco in his cheek. Propping his worn boots on the desk, he settled in to wait.

Em struggled to wake up from a nightmare. In the dream, she was locked in a room with old linoleum on the floor. Scuffmarks covered every square inch, and she scrubbed and scrubbed but couldn't get them out. She pounded on the door and yelled for someone to let her out. A key turned in the lock. She backed up and waited for it to open. The grim reaper filled the doorway, wearing a long black robe and holding a vicious-looking sickle.

Silently screaming, Em jerked awake. Her heart jumped crazily in her chest. She looked at the young woman asleep in the rocking chair and recognized her as the girl who had been in the room earlier. Em recalled the girl being called Abby.

Her head throbbed, but did not feel as painful as before. She reached behind her head to feel the bump. It was tender to her touch. Em tried to remember how she had hit her head. All she could recall was a vague feeling of falling. After clearing her throat, she croaked out Abby's name.

Snapping out of her doze, Abby's warm brown eyes smiled at Em. "Feeling any better, Emily Grace?"

"Yes. But I still can't remember how I got here."

Abby rose from the rocker. "Well, now that you've rested, you can ask me whatever you like. But first, let me help you sit up."

Abby looped her arms under Em's armpits and pulled her upright. Then she propped two pillows behind her back.

"Man," Em said, "you sure are strong."

Abby's forehead wrinkled. "Did you call me a *man?*"

"No."

"Then why did you say it?"

"*Man* can mean 'wow.' "

"I do not understand the word *wow* either."

"What word would you use to express surprise?"

Abby thought for a moment. "I guess I would say *golly.*"

Em barked out a laugh. "Only my great-grandmother uses that word. She's ninety-three years old."

Abby looked slightly offended, and Em was sorry she'd made the remark. "What is your great-grandmother's name?"

Em concentrated, but couldn't come up with an answer. "I can't even picture her."

Abby returned to the rocker. "Since you can't remember much about yourself, let me tell you about me. I am sixteen years old. I abide in Richmond and have been visiting with my aunt for the last few weeks."

Adjusting the pillows until they were more comfortable against her back, Em inquired, "What's *abide?*"

"Where you live."

Em said, "No offense, but I don't get some of the things you say."

Abby peered at Em. "I take no offense. Your accent is rather peculiar. There is a bit of the South in it, but you talk like you're from the North or the uncivilized western states."

Abby looked from Em's face to her clothes. "Do you know why you are clad only in your *under things?*"

Em pulled back the covers. She could not remember having put on these clothes. "What do you mean by under things?"

"You do not have on your slips, corset, crinoline, or dress. You must have come to this house from outdoors, yet you wear no outer garments."

"No, I don't know why." Em pulled the covers back over her waist.

"Perhaps someone broke into your home before you were attired for the day, and you ran away, fearing for your life. There have been a few home intrusions by ruffians."

Em figured that was as good a possibility as any. "But why did I hit my head on your mantle?"

"Oh, Moses startled you, and you tripped."

"Who is Moses?"

"Rachael's husband." Abby jerked upright. "Oh, where are my manners? You have not partaken of any food. May I get you something to eat?"

Em's stomach rolled in a queasy motion. "No, thank you. My stomach—"

Abby jumped up. "I will inform Rachael. She will make you a marvelous ginger tea."

Before Em could answer, Abby picked up the empty cup on the bed stand and left the room.

Em closed her eyes, wondering who she was and where she lived.

Robert gave his wife a lingering hug as Corporal Hinkle opened the makeshift prison's door. He watched her back until the door was shut and locked, wishing their visits could be longer—wishing even more that he could be home with her.

"Sir."

Robert turned at the sound of Hinkle's voice.

"Bowers and I would have a word with you."

Robert found it interesting that Hinkle called him *sir*. He had never used that term before. Though never outright offensive, Hinkle and Bowers had made it clear that they held the prisoners in the utmost contempt. They resented the duty of babysitting "rebel scum."

Robert raised his eyebrows in a questioning gesture.

"Just a word, sir, in the office." Hinkle motioned with his rifle.

Curious, Robert preceded Hinkle into the small room.

Bowers rolled a bit of tobacco in a small piece of dirty white paper while Hinkle kept the gun pointed at Robert. Pinching both ends of his cigarette, Bowers stuck one end in his mouth and lit the other with a strike of his match on a flint strip. After taking a deep draw on the cigarette, he causally blew out the smoke. "Care for a bit of a smoke, Captain?"

"No, Sergeant, I prefer a good cigar. You had a question for me?"

Bowers studied Robert through a drifting haze of smoke. "So, Chamberlain, how do you feel your treatment has been at Hotel McCulloch?"

Hinkle guffawed.

Bowers' dark eyes stared at Robert.

"Well?" Bowers said.

"No complaints," Robert replied cautiously.

"Good." Bowers took another pull on the cigarette. "Hinkle and I have a proposition for you that would be to our mutual benefit. Seeing as how we've treated you so fairly, we figure you owe us a little compensation."

A proposition? What were they talking about? Robert thought.

"You know the whereabouts of the rebel gold. You were on the train with it when it left Richmond, and nobody's seen hide nor hair of it since Davis was picked up." Bowers raised his hand before Robert could argue. "Don't try to deny it."

They thought he knew where the monies from the confederate treasury were hidden. Robert shook his head.

"Now, this is the way it's going to play out. Hinkle and I are due to be discharged after you are pardoned. The three of us will take a little trip to the gold, where we will split it fairly and then go about our business."

Dancing on my dead carcass, Robert thought. "Let me see if I have this straight. I take you to where the gold is hidden, commit treason by stealing it since it belongs to the U.S. government, split it with you two fine gentlemen—and I use the phrase loosely—and then try to spend it."

Angrily crushing his cigarette out on the corner of the desk, Bowers rose to his full height, eyeball to eyeball with Robert. "Listen to me, you rebel scum. You will take us to that gold or my name ain't John Bowers."

Robert did not back away. "I have no knowledge of the final destination of that gold. I suggest you direct your inquiries to the secretary of the treasury."

Bowers drew back his right arm and sucker-punched Robert in the stomach with a fist the size of a ham hock. The air exploded from Robert's lungs, and he dropped to one knee on the wooden floor. Desperately trying to draw in air, he barely heard Bowers' next statement.

"You have until next Wednesday to see the error of your ways. If you don't, you or one of your loved ones will suffer the consequences."

Slowly, Robert rose to his feet. With his left arm held protectively across his stomach, he glared at Hinkle and Bowers. "General Hartsuff frowns heavily on prisoners being beaten."

Looking around the factory floor, Hinkle snickered. "Well, looks like to me we're all out of generals here."

Bowers's merciless eyes stared into Robert's. "You are dismissed, Captain Chamberlain. You've been warned."

Furious at his helpless situation, Robert returned to his cot.

Sarah smiled as her skirts disturbed the dirt along the edge of the road back to her home. "Only five more days, Moses. It feels like an eternity that Captain Chamberlain has been locked up."

"Yes, Missus. I shore will be happy to have da Mista back."

"And I apologize for that rude guard's behavior toward you."

"I don' pay it no never mind. It's da way most white folk talks to us coloreds."

"Well, it is still disrespectful."

Silence fell as Sarah's thoughts turned to the young girl in Abby's bed. What could be so horrid as to send a young lady sneaking into an unfamiliar home in her undergarments? And could Emily Grace's troubles follow her to the Chamberlain home? Despite Robert and Abby's confidence in her, Sarah did not know if her decision to let Emily Grace stay was the right one.

The driver of a buckboard wagon hailed them as he slowly rumbled past. Sarah dipped her head in acknowledgement of the greeting.

As she turned onto the pathway to her house, her shoes crunched along the oyster-shell walkway. On the front porch, she shook the road dust from her skirts. Moses disappeared around the back of the house. Sarah pulled the small ring of keys from the large pocket of her dress. She chose one and swiftly, unlocked the door, stepped inside, and relocked it behind her. She slipped the keys back into her pocket. Sarah trusted Rachael and Moses enough to keep the various cupboards and cabinets unlocked and did not believe that Emily Grace would steal anything. Besides, her most valuables possessions—fine china, silver, crystal, jewelry, etc.—had been hidden away a few years ago because of the war and would not be retrieved until Robert's return.

Untying the ribbons of her hat, she placed it on the mahogany stand with her shawl and gloves. As she patted a few stray hairs back into place, Rachael appeared at the top of the kitchen stairs with a porcelain cup of something steamy and handed it to Abby, who balanced it on a small tray.

"Hello, Aunt Sarah. Emily Grace is awake but has a little stomach problem. I am taking her some ginger tea." Abby walked toward her aunt.

"Does she remember anything?"

"No, ma'am, but I do not believe she is from Petersburg. Her vocabulary is quite strange. She used some words I did not comprehend. And she believes the word *golly* to be quite old-fashioned."

"How interesting." Sarah followed Abby up the stairs to the bedroom, where they found their guest staring listlessly out the window. She turned when the two women entered the room.

"Here is your tea, Emily Grace. Drink it slowly, for it is quite hot."

Taking the cup from Abby, she put it to her lips and took a tentative sip. Abby was right; it was hot, but it didn't burn her tongue. The tea had a bitter quality even though there was some kind of sweetener mixed in. "I don't remember much, but I'm quite sure I've never tasted this kind of tea before."

"It should help your stomach feel better soon," Sarah said.

Sarah sat in the rocker. "Do you recall anything about yourself?"

Holding the cup in her lap, Em closed her eyes. After a few minutes, she opened them and slowly shook her head.

"Tell Aunt Sarah about the breakthrough you had about your great-grandmother," Abby said.

"It just came to me that she used to say *golly* a lot."

Sarah sat back in the rocker. "Well, that is a start. I should consult with Doctor Woods to beg his advice." She looked at Em. "But first, you must put on some proper clothing. I have a dress I have been altering that I think may fit you, although it will be a little short because of your height."

Sarah turned toward Abby. "Darling, could you bring me the dress beside the sewing machine?"

As Abby left to do her bidding, Sarah turned back to Em. "I am certain your memory will return in a few days. Abby and I have prayed for you, and our God is quite faithful."

Emily Grace's lips pinched together. For a brief moment she felt anger, but then the feeling disappeared. Sarah was startled at the change of expression on the girl's face.

"Surely you do not blame our Father in heaven for this unfortunate episode?"

"No, I . . . I don't think I do." Emily Grace hesitated. "I'm sure you're right that He will take care of me somehow."

Abby reentered the room and handed the dress to Sarah.

Emily Grace's eyes popped wide. "That is the most beautiful dress I have ever seen."

It was a lovely shade of jade green. Attached to the collar and cuffs was pristine white lace. The bodice was pleated, with little ebony buttons running down the front. The hem was gathered at the bottom with little black bows; a bit of the same white lace peeked through the gaps in the material. She tentatively touched the lace on the collar and cuffs.

Sarah smiled. "It is fortuitous that I finished the alterations the same day you graced us with your presence."

Em shook her head. "I'm not sure I would call it *grace*."

The rocker creaked as Sarah rose. "You finish your tea and rest. Rachael will be up in an hour or so with some soup." She turned to Abby. "Would you take this dress to Rachael to have it pressed? I think I will retire to my room until dinnertime."

"Of course, Aunt Sarah." Abby accepted the dress, and both turned toward the door.

"Mrs. Chamberlain?"

Sarah turned back toward Emily Grace. "There is no need to be formal, please call me Sarah."

"Thank you for all the trouble you've gone to for me."

"It is my Christian duty, and I would have it no other way."

Em watched the two women leave the room. Bringing the cup to her lips, she sipped the tea. It slowly settled the nausea in her stomach. She almost felt normal. That thought made her laugh because she had no idea what *normal* was for her.

After a two-hour nap, Rachael brought in a tray with a bowl of steaming soup. The aroma was heavenly. Rachael placed the tray on her lap. Square in the middle was a pink bowl, which matched the teacup she had drunk from earlier. Small bits of vegetables and chicken floated in a yellow broth. It tasted delicious, as did the accompanying piece of dark bread. While she ate, Em drank another cup of the willow-bark tea.

When she finished eating, Em sighed in contentment. *Nothing like a good bowl of soup to chase away gloomy thoughts.* Someone had said that to her, but who? Em picked up the last piece of homemade bread and savored the morsel. As if sensing when Em would be finished, Rachael reappeared at the door.

"Rachael, that was absolutely wonderful. You are a totally awesome cook!"

Rachael picked up the tray. "Thank you, Miz Emily Grace. You looks to be feeling a heap better."

"I am. But could you tell me where the bathroom is?"

"Bathroom? I ain't shore what you' mean?"

Racking her brain for another way to say it, Em came up with another phrase from her great-grandmother. "I need to relieve myself."

"Oh, shore. Da potty chair is over in da corner beside da warshstand. Rags fo' wipin' be there too."

Em had no idea what Rachael was talking about. But she didn't bother asking. She could figure it out herself.

Rachael set the tray on the walnut dresser against the wall. "You jus' hold on to me, an' I will help you to da potty chair."

Em's face flushed in embarrassment. "I'm sure I'll be fine."

"Miz Emily Grace, you is gonna be dizzy when you tries to stand. Lemme help you." Throwing back the covers, she eased Em's legs over the side of the bed. When her bare feet hit the floor, Rachael pulled her slowly to the edge of the bed.

That was when Em realized Rachael wasn't kidding around. The room swam viciously. Em swallowed hard, determined not to throw up. Once the pieces of furniture swam back to their proper places, Em tried standing. Letting Rachael take the bulk of her weight, she eased to her feet. She waited a few seconds before taking an exploratory step. Cautiously, she made her way toward the walnut washstand with a white marble top.

Rachael opened the cabinet doors and brought out a couple of rags. Em thought she would die of embarrassment if Rachael insisted on staying while she relieved herself.

"I'm okay now. You can take the tray back."

Rachael looked at Em with amusement. "I don' know why you makin' such a fuss 'bout peeing in dat pot, but iffen you want to be private-like, dat's okay wif me."

After Rachael left and shut the door behind her, Em turned her attention to the potty chair. She was positive she had never used one before, but when she tried to conjure up an image of what she had used, all that came to mind was a large ceramic bowl with smiling bubbles swirling around inside. *Well, that's just ridiculous.* Em shook the image away.

Ten minutes later, Em collapsed back on the bed with perspiration popping out on her forehead. She wished desperately for a fan. Within a few minutes, she fell asleep.

After their meal, Sarah and Abby went up to check on Emily Grace. Sarah put the light cotton sheet over the girl's sleeping form. "You can sleep with me tonight, Abby, so you won't disturb her slumber."

Rachael arrived to empty the chamber pot as Abby untied the mosquito netting from the bedposts so that it draped the sides of the bed. Abby quietly pulled her nightgown from the dresser drawer and followed her aunt from the room.

Chapter Nine

Sunday June 18, 1865

Em slowly opened her eyes and listened to birds chirping merrily somewhere outside her window. Smiling, she turned over and burrowed into her soft nest. Just a few more stolen minutes of sleep before she had to get up and . . . and do what? She couldn't remember what she should be doing. The events of yesterday came flooding back.

Sitting up groggily, she stared at the mosquito netting until her bladder made its urgency known. Pushing the net aside, she rose and padded across the floor.

Just as she finished, there was a knock on the door.

"Come in."

Rachael bustled into the room, wearing the same faded brown dress, long apron, and floral scarf as the day before. Frowning, Em thought, *"It's not a scarf; it's a kerchief."* The kerchief wrapped around Rachael's head, ending in a knot high up on her brown forehead. In Rachael's hands was a pitcher of warm water, which she poured into the ceramic bowl on the washstand.

"How is you feelin' dis fine morn, Miz Emily Grace?"

Em thought about it for a moment. "I feel pretty good. No headache or bellyache, thanks to you."

Rachael smiled. "Well, now, dat's mighty fine. Missus Sarah will be pleased. I'll be right back wif some rinsing water. You go ahead an' wash yo'self. Soap and sponges be in da right drawer."

Feeling a bit self-conscious, Em dropped her baggy capris by the bed and took off her baby-doll top, laying it on the bed. After crossing to the washstand, she opened the drawer and extracted a sliver of what she assumed was soap. An image entered her mind of a white bar of soap with the word *Ivory* in the middle, but it quickly disappeared. Shrugging, she dipped the soap in the water and lathered it into a light brown sponge with holes in it. The aroma of lavender rose to her nostrils. Starting with her face, she scrubbed her lean frame.

Just as she finished, Rachael appeared with the pitcher in one hand and underclothes slung over her other arm. "Lawsy me, child, what you wearin'?"

Em looked down at herself. "A bra and panties."

"I never seen da likes o' dat before." Rachael shook her head. "Never you mind—we's got to git you bathed an' dressed." After placing the clothing on the bed and the pitcher on the washstand, she took the bowl to one of the open windows and tossed the soapy water onto the ground. When she'd put the bowl back on the stand, she poured in fresh water and handed Em a new sponge. Once she was rinsed off, Rachael handed her a clean towel from the cabinet shelf.

Indicating she would return in a few minutes, Rachael left the room again. She came back with the green dress, which had been freshly ironed, and small black boots.

She explained that Missus Sarah had instructed her to help Em dress. Strangely, Em didn't feel as anxious about being dressed as she had about using the potty chair. She felt as if she had gone through this ritual before.

Rachael indicated that Em needed to remove her underwear, and blushing, she complied. The drawers were made of light cotton. A camisole of the same material went over her head. Rachael wrapped a lightweight corset made of whalebone around Em's torso and hooked it into place.

After putting on the under slip, Em stepped into the crinoline. Rachael tied it tight around her waist then slipped a white cotton petticoat over it. Rachael carefully gathered up the dress and dropped it over Em's raised arms, then buttoned up the bodice. Stepping back, she eyed the dress critically. "Well, it be a little loose and a mite short, but it'll do."

Rachael pointed at a wooden chair beside the dresser and told Em to sit so she could do her hair. After three unsuccessful tries at sitting in the hoops under her skirt, Em looked at Rachael helplessly.

"Lord, child, didn't yo' mama teach you nothin'?"

Rachael demonstrated how to collapse the hoops in the crinoline so Em could sit. Em copied Rachael and felt the crinoline give way beneath her.

Rachael rummaged through a dresser drawer for hairpins. Placing them beside the hairbrush on top of the dresser, she turned her attention to Em's hair.

Rachael stared in bewilderment. "You got somethin' caught in yo' hair."

Reaching behind her head, Em's hand came in contact with the elastic band she had used to keep her hair out of her face. She removed it and slipped it over her wrist without even thinking about it.

Rachael deliberated on the best arrangement for Em's heavy mane. Her hands moved deftly as she brushed out the tangles, parted Em's hair down the middle, and gathered locks from either side of her face, twisting them behind her head and securing them with the hairpins. Rachael twirled the stray pieces beside Em's ears around her finger, then released them slowly.

"Not quite the curl you git wif da curlin' iron, but dat be fine." Stepping back, she grinned. "You shore do have da purtiest shade of red hair, Miz Emily Grace."

Em thanked Rachael as the woman returned to the bed and picked up a pair of white stockings and the boots. Lifting Em's right foot, she slid on one of the stockings, repeating the procedure with the left foot. Next came the leather ankle boots. They looked a little small, but Em found she could wiggle her toes as Rachael laced them up. As she helped Em rise off the chair, Sarah and Abby entered the room, dressed exactly as they had the day before.

Abby clapped her hands in delight. "Emily Grace, you look splendid."

As both women exclaimed over Em, Rachael crossed to the bedside to pick up Em's discarded clothing. As she picked up the beige capris from the hardwood floor, Rachael did not notice the old leather diary drop to the floor from the pants' pocket. She laid Em's clothing on the rocking chair then returned to tighten the screws on the rope bed frame. Her foot kicked the diary under the bed. Once the ropes were tightened, Rachael straightened the bedcovers and tied back the mosquito netting. Finally, she tossed out the dirty water and left the room with the chamber pot.

Tugging on Em's arm, Abby pulled her to the mirror that rested on the dresser's marble top. "Emily Grace, you are an absolute vision." She grabbed the top of the mirror, swiveling it to the right angle for Emily to see most of her form.

Em sucked in her breath. She did look beautiful. Her wavy hair fell softly past her shoulders, except for the pieces secured with hairpins. The hue of her dress made her green eyes more vivid. Em couldn't remember ever feeling this way before. Turning around, she looked over her shoulder to try to see the back of the dress.

"Colonel Jacob's trunk of clothes has been a godsend," Sarah said. "Without it, I would have had nothing with which to dress you."

Em looked closely in the mirror and caught sight of the scar on her neck. *How did I get that?* Her smile faded.

Noticing the distressed look as Em gazed at her neck, Sarah said, "I have a black satin ribbon that would look lovely around your neck," Sarah said. "Come with me."

Em followed Sarah to the bedroom across the hall. It was twice the size of Abby's. The floor space must have covered one whole side of the house. An ornately carved mahogany bed sat against the wall opposite the fireplace, covered with a multicolored bedspread in a paisley print. On the floor between the bed and the fireplace was a deep burgundy carpet with colorful flowers woven intricately throughout. Next to the bed were twin nightstands with marble tops and oil lamps with opaque glass globes. A sewing machine sat under one window next to a needlepoint chair and a hand-carved mahogany rocker. A portrait of a man, a woman, a teenager, and a young child hung over the fireplace. Em cocked her head to the side as she gazed at it. *Something about that portrait . . .*

"Emily Grace?"

Em looked at Sarah. "This room is cool."

"Cool?" Sarah and Abby asked with the same puzzled look.

Em giggled. "I'm sorry. *Cool* is a compliment."

Sarah smiled. "I would very much like to learn more of your strange phrases."

"No sweat." Em grinned. "And that means, 'No problem.'"

Abby wrinkled her nose. "That phrase is disgusting."

Em laughed.

"When you receive your memory back," Sarah said, "I will be fascinated to know where you learned your colorful language."

"Me too." Em cleared her throat. "I mean, 'So will I.'"

Sarah held out a piece of ribbon with a small cameo pinned in the center. Em lifted her hair off the back of her neck, and Sarah's warm fingers tied the ribbon at the nape of Em's neck.

Em fingered the cameo as tears trembled on her lower lashes. "Thank you for taking care of me."

Sarah was touched. "You are quite welcome, my dear." Sarah studied Em's earlobes. "I like the little diamond studs you're wearing."

Em reached up and touched the studs as Sarah turned towards the door.

"Ladies, we will spend a few moments in the back parlor before our morning meal."

Em followed Sarah and Abby to the parlor at the rear of the house. A feeling of trepidation overcame her as she crossed the threshold. "Is this the room where I fell?"

Sarah gave Em a curious look. "Yes, it is. Are you remembering something?"

"No. I just got an odd feeling when I saw the room."

Sarah pointed to the needlepoint chair by the fireplace. "Pray, sit down and close your eyes. Something may come to you."

Clumsily trying to maneuver around the card table with her skirts, Em finally sat in the chair as Rachael had taught her. She closed her eyes and tried to access any memories. "I'm sorry. I'm not getting anything." But I am sure I have never been around anyone, except my great-grandmother that talks in such a totally old fashioned way." She continued, "And I don't mean that to be offensive."

Sarah repeated, "Old-fashioned. Abby mentioned that *golly* is not a word you use. But where could you have abided where the language spoken was so different from ours?"

When Em just shook her head, Sarah continued. "I'm guessing you must be from one of the big northern cities, perhaps New York. The language there tends to be diverse due to the influx of immigrants from all over the world."

Abby grinned. "I wonder if you could be the daughter of a missionary and you picked up odd sayings from overseas, maybe in Africa or the West Indies."

Rachael entered the room and said breakfast was ready to be served. Glancing at the clock on the mantle, Em noticed the time to be nine o'clock.

"What day of the week is it?" she asked Sarah as she grasped the arm of the chair to rise.

"Why, it is Sunday. We planned on having you accompany us to worship service." Sarah paused. "Although I should not presume—."

"I would like to go with you."

"Splendid!"

In the dining room, Em pulled out a cushioned chair opposite Sarah and Abby. She noticed a corner cabinet, which held pieces of the pink china that graced the table. It seemed familiar, but Em didn't know why. Looking through the doorway at a portion of the front parlor, she had exactly the same feeling as she spotted two gold satin-tufted chairs But how could they since she had never seen them before?

Rachael entered with a large wooden platter heaped with pancakes and ham.

Sarah's eyes widened in shock. "Rachael! Where did you find flour and ham?"

Rachael set the platter down between the women. "Yesterday at da sutler's, dey sold some to us colored women 'cause they had more than they needed for da soldiers."

"How splendid! I haven't had flapjacks in over two years."

Em was confused about all the fuss. "Why not?"

"Well, because of the war, of course."

"What war?"

Rachael poured coffee into cups from a pewter pot. Sarah waited until Rachael filled each cup with chicory coffee before answering Em's question.

"I will answer your question after we say the blessing." Bowing her head, Sarah gave thanks to "our blessed Lord" for the "eatables" provided by His loving hand. When she'd finished, she put her napkin in her lap and turned to Em. "There was a war between the northern and southern states over states' rights. The northern states won, and our city of Petersburg is under occupation rule."

Em's eyes widened. "When was this war?"

"It began in 1861 and ended in April of this year."

"And what is today's date?"

Abby lifted two flapjacks and a piece of ham off the platter with a large metal fork. "June 18th, 1865."

"Oh." Em helped herself to three flapjacks and two pieces of ham, then took a sip of the coffee. Grimacing, she set it back on the saucer. "That's gross."

"Gross?" Sarah shook her head. "Never mind."

Abby passed the pewter sugar bowl. "A little of this will help sweeten the bitterness."

Em put in a full teaspoon and started to spoon up another when Sarah stayed her hand. "We are on rations, dear, and sugar is precious."

Em's face flushed as she removed her hand from the spoon. "I'm so sorry. I didn't know."

Sarah smiled. "That's all right. Do not concern yourself."

The rest of the meal passed in pleasant conversation. As the platter and plates were removed, Sarah announced the need to put on their outdoor attire because her cousin Beatrice would soon arrive with her buggy.

At the hallstand, Sarah draped an intricately laced black shawl about Em's shoulders and handed her a pair of black cotton gloves. Em put a black straw bonnet on her head and tied it as she saw Abby do with her own bonnet.

Sarah and Abby each picked up a reticule. Both were embroidered and beaded. Sarah's depicted a scene of birds in a birdbath, and Abby's had a little cupid on it. Sarah apologized that she did not have one for Em. She did, however, have a small fabric fan for each of them.

All three women, appropriately attired, passed through the front door and into a mild morning with nary a cloud in the sky. They'd just begun walking down to the dirt road when a black buggy pulled to a stop before them. A statuesque woman in her mid-fifties, with salt and pepper ringlets framing a heart-shaped face, gazed at Em from the driver's seat of the buggy. Dressed all in black, she had worn her widow weeds since the death of her wealthy husband six years prior.

With a twinkle in her eye as she gazed at Em, Beatrice said, "So, what have we here, dear Sarah—a companion for Abby?"

"This is Miss Emily Grace. I will apprise you of her story on the way to the church."

The buggy dipped a bit as Sarah placed her boot on the step to enter. Adjusting her skirts, she settled on the black leather upholstery beside Beatrice in the front of the buggy. Abby and Em sat on the back cushion. Beatrice tugged on the reins, and the horse made a wide turn in the middle of the road, proceeding down the street at a brisk gait.

Em stared, fascinated at the brick town homes they passed as the conveyance creaked beneath her.

As the buggy approached a crossroads, Em gasped at the sight before her. Buildings displayed battered fronts and jagged brickwork. The paneless windows looked like mouths open in horror at the devastation around them.

Abby touched her hand. "Do you remember viewing any of this destruction?"

Too shocked to utter a word, Em merely shook her head.

Beatrice turned right onto Market Street.

"All the horses belonging to the town's people were confiscated for the war effort, and very few have been replaced," Abby explained. "Beatrice is one of only a handful of the citizens of Petersburg who could afford to purchase a horse after the war ended." Many buggies sat idle behind their owners' dwellings.

Beatrice pulled the brown bay to a stop in front of the wrought-iron fence at Saint Paul's Episcopal Church.

"This is my church!" Emily squealed.

A couple climbing the stone steps of the church turned to look at the young woman shouting in the buggy.

Practically bouncing up and down on the seat's cushion, Em stared at the edifice. She didn't recall the stucco being such a dark brown, but it was definitely her church.

"Perhaps someone will recognize you," Abby exclaimed.

The couple entered the church as the ladies descended from the buggy. Beatrice tied the reins to the hitching post as Sarah turned to Em. "Is there anything else you remember?"

"Only that I have been attending here since I was a child." A new thought took hold. "I must have parents who attended with me. Maybe they are in there, praying for my safe return!"

Before Sarah could stop her, Em bolted for the stairs, climbing as fast as she could with both fists clutching handfuls of her dress so she wouldn't trip. The large wooden door was heavy, but she managed to pull it open.

The atmosphere inside was hushed, with a few whispered conversations reaching her ears. She recognized the vestibule with its four brocade chairs, one in each corner. Crossing into the sanctuary, she scanned the people seated in the wooden pews for a familiar face. Not recognizing anyone, her excitement faded.

Em heard Sarah whisper behind her, "Emily Grace must be mistaken about this being her church. I have attended here for five years, but I have never seen her here."

"And I have attended since Saint Paul's opened its doors," Beatrice added.

Abby murmured. "I have not noticed her since I have been visiting."

The three women joined Em as she stared at the opaque glass that graced the eight large windows. "Where's all the beautiful stained glass?"

On both sides of the church, opaque glass graced the eight large windows. As she looked toward the front, she gasped in shocked dismay.

Beatrice asked, "What, child? What is wrong?"

With a finger visibly trembling, she pointed at the wall behind the baptismal fount and pulpit. "And why did they build a wall in front of the choir loft?"

Sarah put a comforting arm around Em. "The choir loft is in the balcony."

Looking up, she saw empty wooden benches. "But . . ."

"It's all right, Emily Grace." Sarah led her to the nearest pew and helped her sit. "The three of us believe this is not your church after all—just very similar to the one you must attend."

"But I could have sworn it was my church."

"Sworn?" Beatrice gasped.

Sarah and Abby shook their heads, and Beatrice clamped her mouth shut.

As the bells chimed, Sarah noticed Doctor Woods and his lovely wife enter the sanctuary. Excusing herself, she walked over to the doctor to ask his advice about Emily Grace.

Em continued to glance around the sanctuary in total confusion. Soon after Sarah's return the procession began, led by the reverend in his priestly robes. As the Reverend William Pratt approached their pew, Em had no idea that her ancestral uncle was gliding by just a foot away. Without a second thought, Em bowed her head and prayed for her memory to return soon. Em had no trouble following the directives in the service, only faltering on a hymn she did not know. How could this familiar place not be her church?

After the service, as Em shook the reverend's hand and looked into his smiling face, she felt goose bumps rise on her arm.

At the foot of the steps, Sarah and Beatrice introduced her to many of the parishioners, hoping someone could identify her. One gentleman in particular made Abby blush as he strolled their way dressed in an army uniform. He was quite dashing in his powder-blue pants with a yellow stripe down the side and navy-blue jacket with gold lieutenant bars on the shoulders. Hat tucked under his arm, he greeted the ladies with a quick bow. "How are you this morning, ladies?"

Sarah answered, "Quite well, Lieutenant Hackett. May I introduce Miss Emily Grace, who is abiding at our home for a few days."

He smiled at Em. "I am enchanted. Please call me William."

Turning to Abby, who had two rosy spots high on her cheeks, William's smile widened. Placing his hat back on his head, he took her gloved hands in his and stared into her eyes. "Miss Abby, you are as beautiful as always."

Abby removed her hands and lowered her gaze. "Lieutenant, you flatter me."

"It's William, remember?"

Watching the way the sun glinted off his burnt-orange locks and made his blue eyes sparkle, Abby could barely remember her own name, much less his.

"Yes, I remember." She said softly.

As Abby and William talked in low voices, Em noticed a few of the older ladies lingering in front of the church, staring at their group, whispering and frowning. Sarah held her head high, returning stare for stare as if daring anyone to make a comment.

Em wondered what their problem was until she realized that this was the South, and William wore the uniform of a Union soldier. That made him the enemy, and they were in essence consorting with that enemy.

Em looked at Abby and William. *Good for you two.*

Beatrice grinned. "Tea and sweets at my home tomorrow at three o'clock. And I will not take no for an answer." Raising her voice so the eavesdropping old biddies could hear, Beatrice continued, "The war is over, and the sooner some people realize that fact, the better. And we should also celebrate the fact that Robert will soon be returning to your bosom."

Em burst out laughing, but covered her mouth when she noticed the perplexed looks on everyone's faces.

Taking a breath to control herself, Em said, "I am so sorry—please forgive me."

Beatrice turned to Sarah and whispered, "Bump on the head, eh?"

With a quick smile to the group, William said he would be delighted to attend, General Hartsuff's schedule permitting, and bid them adieu until the morrow.

As they climbed into the buggy for the ride home, Abby explained that William was the adjutant for the general. When Em gave her a puzzled look, she explained that an adjutant was like an assistant.

As the clip-clop of the horse's hooves drew them closer to home, Em brooded over the lack of recognition by the parishioners.

Abby squeezed her arm. "Don't worry overmuch. Your memory will come back."

As Em gave her a wan smile, Abby glanced at Em's wrist. "What is that?"

Em looked down. "Oh, that's my hair band. Guess I forgot to take it off."

"Hair band?"

"Yeah. Don't you have one?"

"I have never seen anything like it. Can you show me its function?"

"Sure. How about later tonight? I don't want to mess up my hair now."

"That would be quite acceptable." The buggy gave a sudden lurch around a corner, and Em grabbed the side. Abby's eyes lit with amusement but she didn't laugh.

Robert sat on his bunk, absently running his fingers through his hair as his mind drifted to an evening, over two months ago, fraught with panic.

The treasury building had been in chaos as he and Mr. Trenholm, the Secretary of the Treasury, loaded two heavy trunks onto a flatbed wagon, then joined the driver, who whipped the horses into a frenzied gallop toward the train station. After they careened to a stop, two railroad workers had loaded the trunks, not knowing they had just transferred what little currency was left of the Confederacy into the dark baggage car. Most of it was in useless bills, along with several thousand dollars in gold coins. As the wheels clanked along the tracks, picking up speed, Robert had wanted nothing more than to return to his wife, but President Davis had asked him personally to accompany the secretary on the train to Danville.

When they fled Danville, he hadn't caught even a glimpse of the trunks being loaded, if indeed they *had* been loaded onto the train that began their doomed escape to Georgia.

Agitated, Robert dropped his fingers to his mustache, smoothing down the corners at the edge of his mouth. He couldn't decide if he should tell Sarah about yesterday's conversation with the two scumbags who were guarding him. He didn't want to worry her, but she should be on her guard in case Hinkle and Bowers were insane enough to do something stupid like kidnap his wife.

He jumped up from his cot and paced the floor like the caged animal he was. He could see no way out of his predicament. He couldn't try to escape. Whenever Hinkle went to the privy or out to obtain food, Bowers kept his rifle aimed on Robert's midsection the whole time, and vice versa when Bowers left.

He'd thought about asking the private who brought his meals to request an audience with the garrison major, but the guards no longer let the private in the building. When he knocked, one of them went to the door to receive his meal.

Robert did not want to put Sarah's life in peril by having her go to the major or General Hartsuff. It probably would not make a difference if the major questioned the guards. They would lie, and then it would be two guards' words against a rebel prisoner.

He would probably be dead by morning in an unfortunate "accident." He had no doubt that Bowers could murder him where he sat; he had seen it in his eyes. And what if they believed he had told Sarah where the gold was? A chill settled deep in the pit of his stomach.

With the rifle in his lap trained on the captain, Bowers watched from the office with satisfaction as the captain paced the floor. Chamberlain was worried, and that was good. As he spit a stream of tobacco juice into the spittoon, Bowers's mouth turned up in a grin. The captain was probably thinking about that pretty wife of his and what might happen if someone like him got to her.

A key rattled in the lock, and Hinkle entered with their grub from the mess tent. Right behind him stood the private with Chamberlain's midday meal. Rising to his feet, Bowers locked his big fist around the barrel of the gun and headed for the door.

Before the lad of no more than sixteen could enter the building, Bowers jerked the metal tray from his hands and slammed the door. As Hinkle locked the door, Bowers carried the tray to Chamberlain.

An hour and a half later, the key rattled in the lock again as Hinkle opened the door to the captain's beautiful missus. What he wouldn't give for a few hours alone with this particular piece of fluff. Slamming the door in Moses's face gave him immense satisfaction as he sauntered back to the office to catch two winks.

Sarah rushed to Robert's side, clasping him to her heart. Every bit as ardent, Robert held her like she was his most precious possession.

As they pulled apart, Sarah gazed at his face. "Oh, my love, you look paler than yesterday. Are you ill?"

"No, darling, but I do have information of a serious nature to impart." Robert helped her sit in the chair beside his bunk.

After she pulled off her gloves and bonnet, Sarah grasped his hand. "What is it, my love?"

Lowering his voice, Robert repeated the conversation he'd had with Bowers and Hinkle the day before.

Seeing the worry begin to build in her lovely blue eyes, Robert tried to lighten the situation.

"He is probably bluffing, but I want you to be alert. Lock the doors, and do not travel anywhere unaccompanied."

"I am diligent about locking the front door since Emily Grace's appearance. Moses's presence will deter anyone from approaching from the back door." She gazed into her husband's dear face. "But what about you?"

Robert shrugged his wide shoulders. "They cannot do anything unseemly to me. Rebel or not, there would be an investigation."

Seeing that Sarah was still not convinced, he gently rubbed the fingers clinched against her abdomen. "I will be fine. Now, tell me about your house guest—Emily, isn't it?"

For the rest of her visit, Sarah talked about the enchanting but unusual young girl who was staying with them. Satisfied that he had successfully distracted Sarah from his problems, Robert listened with an attentive ear and laughed at Emily's strange use of words.

"Wherever do you think she could be from?" Sarah asked as she rose from the chair.

"I have no idea, love, but I imagine her memory will return soon."

When their time was nearing a close, Sarah glanced at the guards. "Are you sure I shouldn't apprise the general of their threatening behavior?"

Robert gave her a confident smile. "The general is said to be an equitable man, but I think he would see this as a problem of a trivial nature and simply reprimand the guards. Please don't approach him."

Doubtful that this was a trivial problem, Sarah neverthe-less agreed. Trailing one finger down one of the gray suspenders hooked to Robert's black trousers, she sighed. "Until tomor-row, my love."

Robert kissed the top of her head and echoed, "Until tomorrow."

Chapter Ten

Mid afternoon, Rachael entered the upstairs bedroom and stared at the two napping girls. They had grown up too quickly, doing things white younguns ought not have to do. Miz Abby, her arms coated to the elbows with blood as she helped her daddy at his hospital in Richmond. And what kind of terror did Miz Emily go through to be sent here in her skivvies? Almost adults, they were still as sweet as suckling babes to her tender heart. Because she and Moses had never been able to have children of their own, she mothered those she could. "Miz Emily, Miz Abby, it's time you woke up." When neither girl responded, she raised her voice a bit. "Come on, now, or you won't sleep tonight."

Both girls blinked their eyes and stretched. Abby rose up on an elbow and rubbed her eyes.

Still on her back, Em mumbled, "But Mom, the alarm hasn't gone off yet."

Abby stared at Em. "What did you say, Emily Grace?"

Em frowned. "I think I said something about an alarm."

"The city bells didn't sound," Rachael said.

Em glanced at the nightstand, expecting to see a square black box with glowing numbers on the front showing the time. But there was no clock there.

"You also said *mom*," Abby said. "Does that mean "mommy"?"

Rachael muttered something about the bump on Em's head and shooed both girls out of bed, then helped them dress for dinner.

Stepping off the bottom stair, Em noticed Sarah's bonnet hanging on a peg of the hallstand, which meant she had returned from her visit with Robert.

Abby turned to Em. "I need to visit the privy. Would you ask Aunt Sarah if she needs any assistance from us before dinner?"

Eager to help, Em agreed as Abby hurried to the back door.

As she entered the back parlor, Em found Abby's aunt seated at the writing table. She was writing in a small book with an old-fashioned gold pen. As Em opened her mouth to make her presence known, she noticed the date at the top of the page: June 18th, 1865.

A feeling of dread started in the pit of Em's stomach. It heightened when Em read the first line in Sarah's handwriting. *Oh, diary, I am so grateful. I found out a few days ago that Robert is to be.* . . .

Em's sharp intake of breath startled Sarah, and she looked up. "Emily Grace, you are as white as a ghost." After closing the book, she stood and grabbed Em by the shoulders. "Are you all right?"

Em did not respond as the emotional trauma of the words in the diary tried to connect with her brain and find meaning.

Shaking her slightly, Sarah repeated, "Emily Grace?"

With the pathway to her memories still blocked, no answers came, and Em slowly came out of her daze. Focusing on Sarah, she tried to smile. "I'm sorry. I don't know what came over me."

"You were staring at my diary. Does it evoke some memory?"

"At first I felt something, but now . . ." Em shrugged. "I'm sorry, I didn't mean to pry. Is Robert your husband?"

"Yes. He was on staff with President Davis and was captured in Georgia. He is awaiting parole and will be released Thursday."

"Oh . . . " Em tried to think of the right words to say.

Sarah squeezed Em's arm. "God has been good to me. Robert is alive, whereas other women have not been so blessed." Sarah's eyes brimmed with tears, and she reached into the pocket of her dress for her handkerchief.

It was Em's turn to comfort, and she did what came naturally to her. She folded her arms around Sarah and gave her a tight hug. When Sarah pulled back, she whispered, "Thank you."

The back door opened, and Abby entered the room. Remembering what Abby had asked her to do, Em smiled at Sarah. "Is there anything we can help you with?"

"No, thank you, Emily Grace. Why don't you join Abby as she practices on the melodeon?"

Following Abby into the front parlor, Em looked around. Like the dining room, it seemed familiar. The large room covered the whole first floor on the right side of the house. On the wall across from her was the fireplace with a window on either side.

Em caught her breath as she viewed the picture above the mantle. It was of a stunningly beautiful woman with light blonde hair and the same color eyes as Sarah's. Her eyes seemed to say, *I have a wonderful secret I would like to share.* The wide mouth smiled along with the eyes. She sat in a burgundy velvet chair in a lovely dove-gray gown with her hand resting lightly on the head of the Irish setter sitting on his haunches beside her.

"She's beautiful," Em whispered.

"That is Aunt Sarah's mother, my grandmother. It was painted when Sarah was five years old. She died when Sarah was fifteen."

"I'm sorry. That must have been very hard on her."

"She has endured a lot in the last few years—we all have."

Trying to lighten the mood, Em asked, "Would you tell me about your parents?"

Gracefully sitting on a gold satin sofa across from the fireplace, Abby indicated for Em to join her.

Once they were settled, she answered, "My father, Clayton Alexander, is a surgeon. He is in charge of the Jackson Hospital in Richmond. It can accommodate as many as six thousand patients. My mother, Amelia, is Sarah's older sister by . . . let me think . . . twelve years. We abide in a townhouse in Richmond near the hospital. My brother Richard and I consider the hospital our second home. We were practically weaned on ether."

Em chuckled.

"Richard will leave at the end of the summer for William and Mary to begin studies for his medical degree, and I so wish I could follow."

"Why can't you?"

"It is quite unseemly for a lady to be a surgeon."

"That's ridiculous! Women make fine surgeons."

"You sound as if you know of some."

Em sighed. "I think I do. I just can't remember."

"You must come from a very forward-thinking city. There are no female doctors I have heard of in the South."

Abby rose from the sofa. "I had better start practicing before Aunt Sarah wonders why 'Amazing Grace' is not wafting through the hallway."

Em crossed over a handsome Brussels carpet woven into a diamond motif with gold and brown threads. As Abby took a seat on the bench before the rosewood melodeon, Em was overcome with a sense of déjà vu. She felt that she had stood beside this piano many times, but that was impossible. It must have a twin somewhere, just like the church. *Stranger and stranger*, she thought, like Alice through the looking glass.

Evening twilight illuminated the second-story bedroom as Em watched Abby untie the mosquito netting in preparation for bed. Em ran her tongue over her teeth. They felt fuzzy, and she realized she couldn't remember the last time she had brushed them.

She was dressed in a long, white cotton nightgown, similar to the one Abby was wearing. She wore the "slippers" she had been wearing when Moses found her in the family parlor. Rachael had unbound her hair and given her a nightcap for her head. When Abby finished with the netting, she joined Em.

"Abby, you wouldn't have an extra toothbrush, would you?"

"Oh, my goodness. You do need one. Pray excuse me, I will ask Aunt Sarah." Abby rushed from the room, almost colliding with Rachael, who held a boar's-hair toothbrush in one hand and a large ceramic cup in the other.

Em gasped. "Rachael, you must be psychic."

"Psychic?" Abby mouthed as she walked to the washstand.

Rachael didn't even blink. She had decided to take all the strange sayings and doings around Miss Emily in stride. She handed Em the toothbrush, but Em stared at it in puzzlement. It didn't look like any toothbrush she had ever seen. An image crossed her mind of a pink toothbrush with the word *Colgate* on the side. This one was made out of wood and some kind of animal hair. Telling herself not to be squeamish and that beggars couldn't be choosers, Em looked to Rachael for instruction.

As Abby reached for the toothpowder and her toothbrush on the small shelf above the washstand, Rachael explained the simple technique of brushing her teeth. Abby put her toothbrush over the bowl and put a little powder on the brush, followed with a splash of water from the cup. Putting the toothbrush against the surface of her teeth, Abby started to brush.

Em followed the same procedure. A pleasant peppermint flavor tickled her taste buds. After spitting in the bowl and adding more water to the brush, she shoved it back into her mouth. Abby and Em shared a quick sip of water from the cup and spit into the bowl. Once finished, they dipped their brushes in the cup to rinse them off. The remainder of the water went in the bowl.

Rachael tossed the contents of the bowl out the window and wiped it clean with a rag. "Miz Abby, you wants me to light a candle?"

"No, thank you, Rachael. We are going straight to bed."

"Dat's fine, Miz Abby. Sweet dreams, Miz Emily Grace." Leaving the room, she closed the door softly behind her.

Em pulled the elastic band off of her wrist. "Abby, I'll show you how the hair band works now."

Lifting her auburn hair, Em deftly threaded her hair through the band twice and pulled it tight.

Abby stared in admiration. "Wherever did you find a hair ribbon of such ingenuity?"

"Well, it's not a ribbon. Here, feel it." Em whipped it out of her hair and handed it to Abby. "It's elastic."

Abby pulled on the band. "What is elastic?"

"It's a kind of rubber."

"Like the rubber used for tennis balls and some children's toys?"

"I suppose so. But elastic is more flexible."

She demonstrated by pulling the band wide a few times.

Abby clapped her hands together. "That is amazing. When your memory returns, I should like to know where to purchase one."

As the room darkened, Em set the hair band on the dresser and pulled on the nightcap, tying it beneath her chin.

Abby dropped to her knees beside the bed and bowed her head. Em knelt on the opposite side of the bed.

"Lord," Abby prayed, "we do thank You for this glorious day on Your earthly kingdom, which is now coming to a close. I beseech You on behalf of Emily Grace. Please help her to recall the things she has forgotten so that she may return to the bosom of her family. In Your precious name, we lift up our petitions. Amen."

After pulling aside the netting, Abby slid under the white cotton sheets on the right side of the bed. "I find you quite interesting, Emily Grace. I'm glad you're here."

Em pulled the netting together on her side of the bed and turned to Abby. She could hardly make out her features in the dark. "Me too. Thank you for the prayer. But I'm curious about something. Is it uncomfortable to sleep with all those rags wound in your ringlets?"

"Oh, no, they are quite comfortable."

For a moment, only the sound of the crickets greeting the night could be heard.

Then Abby murmured, "What is it like not to remember who you are?"

Em contemplated the question for a moment. "It's kind of like when you get an itch in the middle of your back, but you can't scratch it. The knowledge is in my brain, but I can't get to it. It's very frustrating."

"Doctor Woods told my aunt it's best if you do not try to remember."

"I know, she told me earlier."

"So we will not speak of it again. Perhaps it will come back on its own."

"Goodnight, Emily Grace."

The next morning, Em asked if she would be washing off again and Abby informed her that they did not bathe every day. Em pulled the nightgown over her head and tossed it on the bed. After removing her under things from the dresser, she dressed quickly in the drawers and camisole. She had just tied the slip around her waist when Rachael bustled in to help. In no time, she had both girls dressed and their hair done.

She told them that Missus Sarah awaited them in the back parlor. Then she picked up both nightgowns and nightcaps, along with Abby's underclothes from last week, and explained that it was wash day.

Entering the parlor, Abby and Em each took a seat on the chairs with the matching floral patterns. Sarah closed a book she had been reading. "Good morning, ladies. How did you sleep?"

"Great," Em said. "Abby doesn't snore like my brother. You can hear him right through the door of his bedroom." Her heart lit up with hope as she realized what she had just said.

"You have a brother?" Abby said.

An image came to Em of a boy laughing and holding a large orange ball in his hands.

Her heart picked up speed from the sudden rush of adrenaline. "Yes, I do! I can picture him in my mind. He is my height, same color of hair and green eyes." Out of nowhere, a name popped into her mind. "And his name is Caleb!"

Sarah smiled. "Doctor Woods was right. If we do not push your memory, it will come back on its own accord."

Em's excitement ebbed. "But that's all I have—just a vision and his name."

"Do not be disappointed," Sarah said. "Every clue brings us closer. I know two Calebs, but they are older gentlemen."

Trying to hide her frustration, Em nodded at the book Sarah had lain on the table. "What were you reading?"

"A book of poetry. Are you interested in literature?"

"I love to read—especially Sherlock Holmes mysteries."

"I have not heard of those stories, but I have a fine adventure story I borrowed from Beatrice. It was published last year: *Journey to the Center of the Earth*. I also have *Wuthering Heights* and *Jane Eyre*."

"I've heard of all three of those, but I haven't read them."

Sarah's eyes sparkled. "The bookcase is in the front parlor. I would be most pleased if you would indulge your passion."

Amused by Sarah's formal way of saying, *"Go ahead and knock yourself out,"* Em pressed her lips tight so she wouldn't giggle. She was about to lose the battle of discretion when Rachael entered the room and said that breakfast was ready.

After they finished eating, Sarah announced that she and Abby would be altering a dress from the trunk of clothes donated to her. Turning to Em, she asked if she would like to help.

Em admitted she did not know how to sew, which Sarah attributed to her loss of memory. She suggested either reading or taking in the fresh air on the rear lawn. Opting for the latter, Em left the dining room for the backyard. She had not really noticed much of the yard the day before on her trips to the out-house in the corner farthest from the house. She had been trying to figure out how to wrestle her skirts practically over her head and not fall in at the same time. She was positive that before she lost her memory, peeing had not been so complicated.

Em noticed Moses pulling weeds from a good-sized garden. She hadn't seen him much the past two days. The sun shone on the small bald spot at the back of his head. Em detected a smile at the corner of his mouth and figured that Moses loved tending that garden.

She descended the steps to the grassy path with worn-down patches of dirt made by many trips back and forth to the garden.

Moses looked up at Em. A dazzling smile burst forth from his coal-black face. "Miz Emily Grace, you shore look a heap better dan you did da otha day."

"Thank you, Moses, for helping me when I conked my head."

"*Conked?*" Moses gave Em a befuddled expression.

"It means 'hit.'"

"Rachael told me you talk kinda different." Moses scratched his bald spot.

"Well, right back at you," Em replied with a grin.

Moses shook his large head. "Is dar somethin' you needs from me, Miz Emily Grace?"

"No. Sarah and Abby are sewing, so I'm just passing time."

"Yes'm." Moses went back to pulling weeds.

Em looked around the yard. It was fairly large, with a plank fence surrounding it. Under a small oak were two white-washed wooden chairs, with a small table painted a daffodil yellow in between. By the back door steps was a hand pump with a black metal bucket beside it. A large washtub sat next to a clothesline. Multicolored flowers bloomed in well-kept borders along the fence line. The vegetable garden occupied a third of the yard in the southeast corner, where the sun could hit the plants continually.

Strolling to the garden, Em looked over the vegetables. She saw oddly shaped tomatoes, cucumbers, beets, radishes, snap beans, corn, and summer squash. Separate from the vegetables was a patch of what looked like herbs and spices. A slight breeze picked up, and two tin plates tied to a wooden stake clanged together, startling her.

Moses chuckled. "You look more scaret dan dat ole crow dat comes here messin' wif my veg'ables." His grin faded quickly. "I mean no disrespec', Miz."

Em laughed. "None taken. Those plates did make me jump."

Em watched Moses work for a couple of minutes. "Moses, how long have you worked for Sarah?"

Straightening to his full height, Moses looked toward the ground. "Bout four years now I's been workin' fo Mista Robert and Missus Sarah."

"Do you and Rachael live here?"

"Yes, Miz Emily Grace. We stay in da basement kitchen."

"You live in a basement?"

Moses glanced up and back down. "We shore do. We has us a nice, soft pallet to lay on at night."

"Where did you live before here?"

"Rachael an me was raised on da Wesley plantation round-about here. We lived dar most of our lives. When Mista Wesley died, he freed Rachael and me. Den we came to Petersburg to live wif Rachael's sister in da colored section o' town an' fine work. When da refugees came, we moved here to watch out fo' Missus Sarah."

"Moses, why do you look at the ground while you're talking to me?"

"I was told by my masta dat be da way of it." Moses shifted slightly on his feet.

"You mean when you were a slave?"

"Yes'm."

Em felt suddenly ashamed, though she didn't know why. "Is this the way you talk to Sarah and Abby?"

"No, ma'am. Missus Sarah and Miz Abby axed me to look at dem when I talks."

"Well, I would like you to look me in the eye too."

Moses looked up. "I was jus' waitin' fo' permission."

"Well, I think that's ridiculous."

"Yes, Miz."

Em pointed to the vegetables. "You're doing a wonderful job with the garden."

"Well, I shore do love it. But we needs some rain. It's been dry near on two weeks now."

Em looked at the cloudless blue sky. "Probably won't be any today."

Aware that she was keeping Moses from his tasks, she said it had been nice visiting with him and strolled over to the chairs under the oak. As she lifted her skirts to sit down, Rachael pushed through the back door, arm muscles straining as she struggled with a cast-iron pot. Moses rushed up the stairs, took it out of her hands, and scolded her for not calling him to bring it up the basement stairs. Carrying the pot as if it weighed nothing, Moses walked to the tub and tipped it. Steaming water cascaded into the tub. Em remembered Rachael saying it was wash day.

Rachael returned to the house and appeared again almost immediately with a woven basket full of underclothes and assorted linens. After setting the basket down by the tub, she walked to the pump and pumped water into the bucket. Moses carried the bucket and dumped it into the tub. After he made two more trips, Rachael poured in some powdered soap from a tin can. Moses filled the bucket one more time, setting it to rest beside the washtub. Reaching into the basket, Rachael selected a few items and tossed them in the tub. After rolling up the sleeves of her dress, Rachael shoved the items under the soapy water. She scrubbed the life out of a pair of drawers against a wooden washboard.

Em watched in fascination. She had never seen clothes washed like this before. A fleeting image came to her of slamming a small white door and turning a knob. But having decided to take Doctor Woods's advice, she let the image go. Instead she concentrated on Rachael as she dropped drawers in the rinse bucket and then hung them on the clothesline with two wooden clothespins.

The warm, gentle breeze made Em drowsy. Just before she gave in to sleep, she heard Rachael mutter, "Now, would you jus' look at Miz Emily's drawers. Dar ain't no slit in 'em. How's she s'posed ta squat and pee?"

The next thing she knew, Josh was smiling at her as he bounced the basketball back and forth between his hands. Em reached out and knocked the ball to her teammate Megan. Running parallel to Megan toward the goal, she caught the ball on its first bounce as Megan passed it to her from behind her back. Em took two big strides, paused, and lobbed the ball into the basket.

From nowhere, Josh leaped into the air, knocking the ball away before it could finish its path into the basket. The ball went flying out of bounds, and Josh grinned at Em as he moved closer to her. The grin disappeared and his face turned serious. He lightly grabbed her arms. "Em, you have to wake up now and remember Robert. Time's running out." Josh's image wavered, and he became transparent. Before he disappeared completely he repeated, "Remember Robert."

Em shook her head and muttered, "Robert." Suddenly, her head snapped forward, causing her to wake up. Blinking her eyes and looking around, she noticed that the clothesline was full of lightly dripping clothes and that Rachael was nowhere in sight.

Em rubbed the back of her neck as she rotated it to get the kinks out. The dream was fading fast, and Em puzzled over an image of a young man with blond hair and a face slick with perspiration. Why had he told her to remember Robert?

The back door opened, and Abby leaned out. "Emily Grace, lunch will be served soon."

"I'll be right there." Em rose from the garden chair and headed for the privy.

Robert waited patiently until the door of the factory prison closed behind Hinkle. Rising from the wooden-framed camp cot, he walked to the office.

Bowers set his chair back on the floor and casually pointed his rifle in Robert's direction. "Something I can do for you, Captain?"

Robert leaned on the doorjamb with a calm he did not feel. "I would like to conduct a transaction that will be profitable to both of us."

Shifting the toothpick he had been chewing to the other side of his mouth, Bowers stared up at Robert. "I ain't going nowhere. Talk."

Robert told Bowers what had transpired the night the money was removed from the Richmond treasury. "So as you can clearly see, I have no knowledge of the whereabouts of the gold coins. But for the safety of my family, I am willing to pay you a goodly sum of money to stop this harassment."

Bowers gave a nasty laugh of disbelief. "You think I'm going to take a few crumbs over the whole loaf? Shut your lying yap and listen up."

Robert knew he was as good as dead if he did not procure the gold.

"I've been doing some thinking, and I don't want to risk you bashing in mine and Hinkle's heads on the road to the gold, so you ain't going with us. And your fibbing confirms that you want that gold all to yourself."

Robert took a step toward Bowers. "You buffoon," he shouted. "Your greed has made you blind to the facts. I am not playing you false. Do I look like the type of gentleman to risk the safety of my precious wife?"

Raising the rifle and aiming it at Robert's chest, Bowers paused before answering. "That gives me an idea. I believe we will take that lovely wife of yours with us on our trip to the stash."

Ice water traveled down Robert's spine. He had to buy time for Sarah and himself. He bowed his head in feigned defeat. "You win. I do not know the location of the gold, but I know who does."

Bowers bared his tobacco-stained teeth like a wild dog. "Now we're getting somewhere."

"His name is Archibald Stephens. He was on the train with me and was pardoned last week in Richmond. If I can get a message to him and tell him it is an emergency, he will come to Petersburg."

Bowers glared, his eyes full of malevolence. "I better be getting that information before you're paroled. If he ain't here by Wednesday afternoon, someone will suffer the consequences."

Realizing that Bowers had swallowed the lie, Robert pressed his advantage. "There is still time for a message to go out on the postal run to Richmond today. Stevens will receive it tomorrow if it is marked *urgent*, and he will come out immediately. I will note in the letter that he needs to be here no later than three on Wednesday."

"Curse your rebel hide." Bowers started to squeeze the trigger.

Seeing that death was imminent, Robert again forced a display of calm. "If you shoot me, you will never find the gold."

Bowers's finger eased off the trigger. "Your friend better know where the gold is, and Hinkle and I had better find it, because if we don't, you will be the sorriest man to ever walk this earth."

Bowers reached into the drawer next to him for a piece of scrap paper and a pencil stub, his eyes watching Chamberlain for the slightest movement. He shoved them into Robert's hand and motioned with the rifle. "Now, get back to your bunk and write that note."

Keeping his face neutral, Robert sagged in relief as he walked back to his cot. He had two days to come up with a better plan, and he'd better think of something. Because Archibald Stephens did not exist.

Chapter Eleven

The three women of 515 High Street strolled down the dirt road to keep their three o'clock appointment for tea with Beatrice. Moses walked behind them with his ever-present stick slung over his shoulder. There was no need for parasols because the only exposed skin was their faces, and the bonnets hooded them.

Unused to the extra clothes the time period dictated, Em was perspiring in several places. She pulled the handkerchief Sarah had given her out of her pocket and wiped sweat off her brow.

"Emily Grace, you don't wipe—you dab." Abby demonstrated the difference with her own handkerchief.

"If Abby has her way," Sarah said, "you will soon have the proper manners of a genteel lady."

"Why are there so many rules? And shouldn't I be remembering *some* of them?"

"You will, Emily Grace." Abby said.

Arriving at Beatrice's townhouse, they looked over their shoulders as hooves sounded behind them. The rider pulled to a stop. "Afternoon, ladies. Ain't you all looking mighty fine?" He gave them an evil sneer.

Sarah heart sped up as she looked up at the pockmarked face of Sergeant Bowers. Moses stepped in front of the ladies, grabbing his stick with both hands.

"Looks like they slapped a little too much shoe shine on you, boy. You better watch yourself with that stick or I just might have to shoot you for threatening a white man."

Beatrice opened her front door at the same time Lieutenant Hackett rode up the street on his black Arabian. Immediately, Bowers' demeanor changed. Sitting up straight in the saddle, he saluted the lieutenant and kicked his horse, setting off at a fast trot.

After dismounting, William Hackett tied his horse's reins to the hitching post. "Was Sergeant Bowers bothering you?"

"He was crass," Sarah said, "but we are not harmed."

"I will have a word with him on the matter."

Sarah paused beside William's horse. "This is a fine animal you have here." She rubbed the gelding's velvety nose. "My grandfather was a horse breeder."

"I acquired him from my uncle's farm in upstate New York." William gave the animal an affectionate slap on the neck. "Now, let us retire to your cousin's parlor and enjoy our tea." He followed the ladies into Beatrice's home.

Comfortably seated on a brown velvet chair with no arms, Em leaned over and whispered to Abby, "What was that about on the street?"

"I do not know."

After Beatrice and Sarah were seated, William crossed to the other side of the room and joined Abby on the settee, leaving a discreet distance between them.

A robust black woman dressed like Rachael entered with a teacart full of cakes and pastries. Em's stomach growled, and Abby laughed before apologizing for her slip in etiquette. Unaware of Em's internal rumblings, both Sarah and Beatrice smiled at the ease William and Abby displayed while in each other's company.

Sarah accepted an apple tart from Beatrice's servant, Gracie, and set it on the table beside her. "Beatrice, wherever did you procure such delightful pastries?"

"From a bakery that recently reopened in Richmond. I had them delivered this morning."

Sarah sipped her tea from a delicate bone-china cup. Using a small silver spoon, she added sugar, stirring it as she spoke. "We do so appreciate these treats, as I do not have the funds for such indulgences."

Beatrice picked up her scone. "Charles was a smart man, dividing his investments between the South and the North when he saw trouble brewing. He left me financially sound." She looked at the cup of tea balanced in her lap. "I do miss him so."

Sarah squeezed her cousin's hand. "I know you do." Sarah swallowed a bite of apple tart. "Has Cousin Townsend heard when General Hartsuff and his staff will be leaving so he can move back into the Bolling mansion?"

"Actually, I talked to him at church yesterday, and it should be in the next couple of weeks." Beatrice took a sip of her tea.

"I do not know whether to be happy or worried that the occupation will be over."

"We needed the Union soldiers to maintain law and order. Otherwise, the criminal element would have wreaked havoc on the citizenship. But the police department has been restored, and I have faith in their ability to keep us safe. No, I am more concerned with the lack of commerce. You don't live with a businessman for thirty-five years and not learn how the economy runs. The ports have been destroyed, along with the rail lines. The tobacco and cotton warehouses are gone. Tobacco and cotton were the heart's blood of this area, and they will not be grown this year, or maybe ever again. With no slave labor—which, of course, I abhor—the landowners must have hired help. They cannot realize a profit in this depressed market." Beatrice sighed. "I am afraid life as we knew it in our fine city of Petersburg is gone forever."

Em bit into her third little cake, this one with strawberries and a dollop of cream on top. Licking the cream from the corner of her mouth, she listened with detachment to William and Abby's conversation.

She tried to remember the young man in the dream she had while napping in the garden. A tingling sensation coursed through her body as she recalled his face. Em felt sure he was someone she had feelings for, maybe even a boyfriend. He was so cute, just thinking about him made her blush.

But she still had no clue why he told her to remember Robert. Sarah had mentioned that her husband's name was Robert. But remembering him made no sense.

"Emily Grace."

Em turned toward William.

"I would like to extend my sympathies on your unfortunate accident which removed your recollections."

"Thank you."

"The headmaster at the school I attended before the war fell from his horse and lost his memory, only to have it return two weeks later. I am sure yours will come back soon as well." He took a sip of his tea.

"From your lips to God's ears."

The cup rattled in the saucer as astonishment crossed William's face. He opened his mouth to say something but apparently thought better of it.

"Emily Grace has a way of phrasing her words that are a bit foreign to our thinking," Abby interjected.

"Actually," William said, "I agree. I believe God does listen to all of our well-meant utterances."

After an awkward pause, Abby said, "I will be returning to Richmond this coming Saturday."

Abby could tell by the twin looks of distress on Emily and William's faces that neither was happy with the news. Both started to protest at the same time, with William, being a gentleman, bowing to Em to go first.

"Abby," Em pleaded, "do you think you could change your plans? I really need you to help me until my memory returns. I didn't even know how to brush my teeth without you showing me."

William's face twisted into such a funny look of puzzlement that Abby laughed, almost upsetting the teacup in her hand.

"She speaks the truth. Emily Grace has forgotten even the most basic things." Abby remarked.

William set his tea on the table beside him and took Abby's free hand. "I am in total agreement with Emily Grace. I beg of you, stay two more weeks. I have so enjoyed your company, and in two weeks' time, the garrison will be moving out, along with the headquarters' staff."

Abby's lower lip quivered. "Where are you going?"

"I am scheduled to travel to Washington with the general. But there are posts that need filling in Richmond. I could put in a transfer if you would be pleased to entertain my company."

Abby looked at their two hands clasped together. "That would please me ever so much."

"Then it is settled. I will put in for the transfer posthaste."

Em still worried about Abby leaving. "Will you stay here a little longer?"

Abby glanced across the room at Sarah before turning to Em. "I will have to speak with my aunt. I had planned to leave in order to give her and Robert time alone when he comes home on Thursday. But with you here, that changes the circumstances a bit."

Em's sighed in relief. "Oh, thank you so much, Abby."

An hour later, William reluctantly kissed the back of Abby's hand and bid everyone good-bye, as duty called him back to headquarters at the Bolling mansion. After he left, the ladies visited for another hour, then Sarah announced that they would have to go since it was almost suppertime. Kissing Beatrice on both of her rosy-red cheeks, Sarah insisted she join them for dinner Wednesday night at six o'clock. Beatrice said she would be delighted.

On the walk home, with Moses's ever-watchful eyes scanning to the right and left of the street, Abby apprised Sarah of the conversation concerning her departure on Saturday. Sarah agreed that Abby should stay for Emily Grace's sake. Em let out the breath she had been holding as she walked beside the two women.

"William seems quite smitten with you . . . and you with him." Sarah said.

Eyes alight with joy, Abby admitted her feelings. "Oh, Aunt Sarah, the way I felt when he held my hand . . . I . . ."

"Felt tingles running through your body?" Em suggested.

Abby shyly admitted it was true. "How did you know?"

"This morning I fell asleep in the backyard and dreamed of a guy with blond hair and a great smile. When I woke up, I had tingles."

Sarah looked at Em. "Do you know who this young man is?"

Em kicked a pebble in the dirt road. "No name came to mind, but I felt that he could be a boyfriend."

"Boyfriend?" Sarah asked. "I have not heard that term before."

Em considered how to explain in a way her friend would understand. "It's used when a boy and girl are committed to each other but not engaged."

When they reached the house, Em noticed the windows to the basement under the porch. Curious about Moses and Rachael's sleeping arrangements, she asked if she might check out the basement. Sarah gave her permission.

Following Em, Abby asked what *check out* meant. Rolling her eyes, Em explained as they entered the house.

After a delicious meal of ham and redeye gravy, green beans, and potatoes cooked in bacon grease, and the ever-present cornbread, Em followed Abby and Sarah into the back parlor. The windows in the room had been lowered and small pieces of mosquito netting strung across the openings, hooked on either side of the window frames.

The netting brought an image to Em's mind. "How cool— homemade screens."

"I beg your pardon," Abby said.

"Screens are like mosquito netting, only stiff. You never take them off the windows. They stay in place all year."

"It was Robert's idea to keep the mosquitoes out of the parlor when we don't have a fire to divert them," Sarah said. "I know he would love to see your screens."

"I'll be happy to show him when I figure out where I've seen them."

"Emily Grace, do you have an interest in playing card games?" Sarah asked.

An image came to Em's mind of a woman with frameless glasses and red hair streaked with gray. The woman was laughing, delighted that Em had won again at a game of Go Fish. "Yes, I do enjoy cards! My grandmother played with me all the time."

"Do you know how to play euchre?"

Shaking her head, Em said she didn't know that one. "But I could teach you and Abby Go Fish."

"That would be lovely. I enjoy learning new games."

Abby and Em spread their voluminous skirts and seated themselves at the card table while Sarah pulled a small box from a drawer of the writing table. Sitting opposite Em, she handed her the deck.

Em looked at the cards in her hands. There were no numbers in the corners. An image of Alice falling down the rabbit hole came to her. "*Stranger and stranger.*"

She looked at Sarah with a puzzled frown. "These cards are weird."

Abby wrinkled her forehead. "I take it that you believe the cards are peculiar in some way."

Sarah's mouth quirked at the corners. "Your colloquialisms are quite different than ours."

"What in the world is coll- . . . coll- . . . kili—?"

Abby laughed. "Colloquialisms are phrases, or part of a conversation."

Shaking her head, Em explained the rules to Go Fish. For the next two hours, Abby, Em, and Sarah played that and other cards games, such as Old Maid and Rummy.

They had just finished a hand when the clock above the mantle chimed eight o'clock.

Sarah sighed. "I am having a marvelous time, but we should be off to bed so as not to use the oil for the lamps."

"You are quite right, Aunt Sarah." Abby rose from her chair and brushed a kiss on Sarah's cheek.

Em felt a longing in her heart for someone to show affection to her like that. She couldn't recall whether a loved one had ever done such a thing with her.

As if reading her mind, Sarah came around the table and stood next to Em. Taking her face gently in both hands, she kissed her lightly on the forehead. "Sweet dreams, Emily Grace."

Tears welled in Em's eyes as she gave Sarah a quick hug and whispered, "Good night."

Chapter Twelve

June 20, 1865

Em awoke on Tuesday morning with a sense of anticipation. While Abby breathed lightly beside her, Em waited quietly to see if her memory had returned. When nothing surfaced, she thought of the word *mother*, hoping for a picture to flash in her mind. None appeared. She sighed in disappointment, but quickly pushed aside the feeling and counted her blessings. She had a nice roof over her head, good food, and women who cared for her welfare. She was truly blessed.

Quietly, so she wouldn't wake up Abby, Em set her sheet aside. The heat had been oppressive during the night, so she hadn't used the quilt. Scooting off her side of the bed, she moved the mosquito netting and slipped her feet into the brown flats on the floor. Tiptoeing, she left the room for the privy. Rachael had brought a changing screen down from the attic to give the girls some privacy while using the potty chair in the bedroom, but Em was still embarrassed to use it when Abby was around.

Lightly descending the stairs, she hoped she wouldn't run into Moses in her nightgown.

After closing the back door behind her, Em looked toward the outhouse. Made of oak and recently whitewashed, it glowed in the early morning dawn. Moses, who loved to work with wood, had carved images of his beloved flowers on all four sides.

Em hurried down the damp footpath and opened the door. Thanks to the dried herbs and flowers that hung from hooks in the ceiling, the tiny room didn't smell too unpleasant. A bucket of lime in one corner also helped.

Em lifted her nightgown and sat on the smooth, sanded seat. Rising a minute later, she thought about how much easier the process was without the multitude of clothes she wore during the day. Aware that Moses could come out the back door at any time, she quickly dumped a scoopful of lime in the hole and hurried across the dew-kissed path back to the house.

Opening the back door, Em almost bumped into Rachael, hands on her hips and a shocked expression on her face. "Honey chile, what's you doin' outside in yo' nightgown?"

"Just going to the privy."

"I done brought dat screen down from da attic fo' you to be private-like."

"Yes, ma'am, I know. It's just . . ."

Rachael looked even more shocked. "You's not s'pose to say *ma'am* to da likes o' me."

"I was raised to address all adults as *ma'am* or *sir*."

Rachael's eyes got bigger. "Even colored folks?"

No specifics came to mind out of the deep, dark void of her mind, but she was still positive this was true. "Yes, ma'am."

Grabbing Em's arm gently, Rachael pulled her into the house and shut the door. Rachael looked up at Em as she tried to decide the best way to explain a way of life that was obviously foreign to her.

"Miz Emily Grace, you mustn't call me ma'am. It's not done hereabouts and it could git you or me in a heap o' trouble iffen da wrong folks overhered."

"Why?"

"Missus Sarah says you be comin' down to da kitchen dis mornin'. I will tell you the way of things then. Now, you scoot back up dem stairs an' I'll be up shortly to help you dress. Da under things you came in is warshed and in da bottom drawer of da dresser." With a light push to her back, Rachael sent Em back up the stairs.

Em climbed the stairs slowly, trying to understand what Rachael had said. Why would someone hurt either of them just because she called her *ma'am*? She felt so confused. Nothing she said or did made sense to the people around her.

Em held her jade skirts in one hand and gripped the rail with the other as she climbed down the narrow stairs to the basement. The huge space, with its hard-packed dirt floor, encompassed the whole underside of the house. An enormous brick fireplace seemed to cover half of the wall to the left. Its cavernous deeps could easily hold two people. The back of the fireplace was black with soot. Hanging on a hook over a low-burning fire was a large cast-iron pot with something bubbling in its depths. Kitchen tools hung on hooks embedded in the brick front. Em recognized tongs and spoons for stirring. Hanging from one of the hooks was an odd contraption that looked like a double set of horseshoes welded to a piece of iron with a long handle. Curious, she pointed it out to Rachael, who stood a few feet away.

"Oh, dat be fo' toastin' da bread." She picked up a slice of bread off of a large wooden worktable and slipped it between the horseshoes. Lifting it by the handle, she slid it over the fire and pulled it out when the toast became a light brown.

"Wow, that is so cool!"

Em's eyes traveled around the rest of the basement. She recognized a jelly cabinet along one brick wall next to a pie safe. Through the glass front of a large kitchen cabinet, Em peered at cooking bowls and pitchers of different sizes. A butter churn stood next to a worktable under the window. On top of the table were piles of vegetables from the garden, chopped and ready to be dropped into the bubbling pot. Bolted to the wall to the right of the window was a double shelf. On it were a copper teakettle, a metal double boiler, and a few things she did not recognize.

Looking to the left of the fireplace, Em spied a pallet barely big enough to fit two people. It looked like a coarse cotton bag stuffed with some kind of material. Spread out neatly on top were a frayed sheet, two plain blankets, and two small pillows.

Two old and scarred rocking chairs stood near the pallet. Next to one were a knitting basket and sewing box. A reddish-brown gourd made into a fiddle lay on the floor next to the other rocker. It had a long handle with four wooden screws at the top to turn the four strings. Em tried to come up with a word to describe what she was observing in the basement. *Primitive* came to mine.

Pointing to a rocker, Rachael asked Em to sit. Once she was settled in, Rachael cleared her throat. "Miz Emily . . ."

"Aren't you going to sit with me," Em asked.

Rachael gave Em a stern look. "What you jus' axed be exactly what I was tryin' to explain. You is a sweet chile and ever so kind. But you gots to know yo' place, like I knows mine. White folks is da privileged ones, and da colored folks take care of da white folks in dar homes an' work places."

Em stared at Rachael with her mouth open.

Rachael softened her stern countenance. "Miz Emily Grace, you gots to stop makin' a fuss 'bout what's right an' wrong. Evens iffen we ain't slaves no more, we gots to stay in our place or we could be whipped or worse. We ain't never gonna be same as white folks."

Em looked at Rachael with determination. "I don't know how I know this, but I am sure that where I come from, white and black folks are equal. They go to school together, work together, and have fun together."

Rachael shook her head. "Dat sounds like a mighty fine place, Miz Emily Grace, but it ain't da way o' things herebouts. You jus' has to be more biddable like to da way things is, precious chile."

Em's eyes welled up with tears that threatened to spill down her cheeks. She rose from her rocker and gave Rachael a fierce hug. "I will try to obey the rules," she said over the woman's hunched shoulder. "I couldn't bear it if you were whipped because of me."

Rachael pulled back and lay her brown hand alongside Em's cheek. "You is a mighty sweet young miz, and I'll be missin' you when you go home."

Rachael took Em's arm and walked her back to the stairs. "Now, you git back up dem stairs to Missus Sarah so ole' Rachael can git back to her chores."

"Yes, m- . . ." Catching herself, Em smiled. "Yes, Rachael. And thank you." Grabbing the railing in one hand and her skirts in the other, she laboriously climbed to the first floor.

Em knocked on the doorframe of Sarah's bedroom and asked permission to enter.

"Oh, please do, Emily Grace." Sarah looked up from her sewing machine. "What was your impression of the kitchen?"

"I don't think mine is anything like it." Sitting in the rocker, Em asked Abby what she was working on.

"Repairing a rip in this corset. Can you see where the whalebone is poking through the material?" Abby held it up for Em's inspection.

After nodding, Em looked around the room, her eyes coming to a halt at the painting over the fireplace. "Sarah, is that a portrait of your family?"

"Yes. It is a picture of my mother, father, my sister, and myself. I was four at the time, and Amelia was sixteen."

"Would you tell me about your family?"

"I would be delighted." Sarah lifted the sewing machine's little foot off the seam of the chocolate-brown dress she was sewing and cut the threads. "I was raised on a plantation a few miles north of Richmond. My great-grandfather, Charles Whitmore, built it in 1791. He grew tobacco. His son—my grandfather, Charles Jr.—expanded the plantation to include horse breeding. My grandfather had a deep love for horses. He married my grandmother, Mary Bolling, because she shared his passion for horseflesh. Beatrice's mother, Anne, was Mary's sister. Charles Jr. and Mary had one child—my mother, Lily. When my mother was eighteen, she met a handsome naval lieutenant, James Langford, at the governor's ball in Richmond. They fell in love, and my father resigned his commission so they could marry and live at the plantation. My father helped my grandfather run the plantation, along with my mother." Sarah's voice grew wistful. "She was a very smart business woman."

Em smiled at Sarah. She thought the history of Sarah's family was fascinating. "My father did not have the same love for horses. He concentrated on the tobacco end of the business. My parents had two children—Amelia and me."

Sarah glanced toward the portrait. Em followed her gaze and studied the family group. They sat on a grassy patch in front of a pasture where three horses frolicked. Little Sarah sat in her father's lap. Amelia snuggled between her parents. Both children looked up at a parent with smiles on their faces. Lily and James gazed at each other with deep affection.

"Your family was very close, weren't they?"

"My mother died when I was fifteen. But the rest of us are still quite close."

"Does your father still run the plantation?"

A sad look clouded Sarah's face. "He was heartbroken when Mother died. He ran the plantation for three more years, until I married. When it became obvious that neither Robert nor I had an interest in running a large plantation, he turned to Amelia and her husband. Amelia's husband is a surgeon and had an established practice in Richmond. They had no interest in taking over the plantation, so my father sold the property. He couldn't abide being in that big house all alone with my mother's memories. Nearly every piece of furniture you see in this house is from my childhood home."

"Where does he live now?" Em asked.

"In a townhouse not far from Amelia. He is quite happy, spoiling his grandchildren shamelessly."

Abby blushed.

"I believe my family is every bit as close as yours." Em folded her hands in her lap. "It's just a feeling, of course."

Sarah put her hand over Em's, and Abby rose to cover Sarah's hand with her own. Both looked into Em's green eyes.

"I have no doubt that is the truth," Sarah said. "I can tell by your morals and your manners that someone has loved you abundantly and turned you into a fine young woman."

"I know that I am repeating myself, but I feel very lucky to have stumbled into your parlor."

"Perhaps it was divine intervention. God watches over all his children." Sarah said.

The loud creaking of the stairs foretold the arrival of Rachael. "Lunch is 'bout ready, Missus Sarah."

"Thank you, Rachael. We shall be down in about fifteen minutes."

"Yes'm." Rachael left the room.

Sarah turned to Em. "And we are just as blessed to have you with us."

Hinkle sat across the desk from Bowers, his rifle trained on Robert. He could sense Bowers studying him. "Chamberlain's wife will be here in a few minutes. When she gets here, I want you to do a little spying. If the reb doesn't come through tomorrow, we may need a little insurance to make him change his mind. Go to the captain's house and look over the windows and doors. Find a way in and out that's real quick. But make sure no one sees your ugly mug."

Hinkle's lips curled into a grin at the prospect. "Are we gonna kidnap one of them females?"

"Ain't nothing gets past you, Sam," Bowers sneered. "But don't go doing anything hasty—I'm only wanting surveillance for now."

At the hard knock on the door, both men looked up. Hinkle grabbed his hat and rushed to the door. He knew right where that fine Southern piece lived.

As he inserted the key in the door lock, he felt Chamberlain's eyes boring holes in his back. Let him glare—he would have the last laugh, and with the reb's own wife.

Pulling the door open, he winked at Sarah. Moses stood behind her, as solid as a statue, his brown eyes fixed on the door as Hinkle passed. For two cents, he would shove his fist into that big, flat nose, but John would have his hide if he did anything to spoil their plans for the gold.

Drawing a filthy handkerchief out of his back pocket, he wiped the sweat off the back of his neck. Shoving it back in his pants, he headed down the dusty road. The pretty woman would want a long visit with her husband. That gave Hinkle plenty of time to poke around their house.

Removing her bonnet and gloves, Sarah hurried to Robert's side and gave him a peck on the cheek.

"The audacity of that man," Sarah fumed. Robert's gray eyes roamed her face. "What did he do?"

"He winked at me."

His countenance turned stony. "That reprobate will be due a reckoning when I am released."

Sarah noticed dark circles under her dear one's eyes that had not been there the day before. "No, Robert, leave him be. In two days, he will be out of our lives."

"Sarah, walk with me to the other end of the building."

As Bowers rose to follow, Robert turned in his direction. "A brief moment alone with my wife, *sir*." The *sir* dripped with sarcasm.

"Five minutes—then back to your bunk."

Once out of earshot, Robert spoke quickly. "Sarah, you must move the household to Richmond no later than two o'clock tomorrow. Beg Beatrice's leave to borrow her buggy. You can stay at Amelia's or your father's residence."

"But Robert—"

"My darling, it is imperative that you do this. I am positive the guards mean you grievous harm. I have fooled them into thinking I have a friend who will apprise them of the whereabouts of the gold tomorrow by three. When he does not appear, they will assuredly go after you or Abby to force my hand."

Sarah gripped Robert's arms. "I will go to the general immediately."

"It would be my word against theirs. I am a rebel prisoner, and they are Union soldiers. They would have to be locked up for you to be safe, and that will not happen without proof. Once I am released, I will talk to the general myself and file charges, but you need to be safely away from here for a few days."

Sarah clung so hard to Robert's arms her knuckles were white. "But what about you?"

"They will not harm me. If they do, they will languish away in a federal prison and will never get the gold they think I have hidden. No, my family is the key to my cooperation, and they know it."

Boot heels stomping on the floor startled Sarah.

"Do not visit tomorrow before you leave," Robert whispered. "It is too dangerous."

"I hate to break up your tête-à-tête, but you could be planning a prison break." Bowers laughed at the absurdity of his comment, then growled, "Get back to your cot."

Grasping Robert's elbow with both hands to help control her shaking, Sarah walked with him back to the other side of the room, praying for God's deliverance from this quandary.

Robert leaned close to Sarah's ear and whispered, "Sweetheart, I think it best if you leave now to prepare for your journey."

Taking a deep breath and steadying her hand, Sarah lifted her bonnet from the cot. After tying the ribbons hastily, she took her gloves from Robert and slipped them on.

He placed both hands on Sarah's shoulders and smiled. "I will be fine. I promise."

"Oh, Robert, I love you so. I would perish if anything happened to you."

"I love you with an abiding love that will never cease. I will come to you in Richmond on Thursday."

His eyes shining with assurance, he led her to the door and kissed her cheek. She gazed at his face for a long moment, not at all confident that she would have the occasion to do so again.

Hinkle whistled as he sauntered down the alley behind the houses on High Street. A Negro child no more than twelve looked up from mucking the stall of the only horse at the stables but quickly averted his gaze.

Hinkle slowed as he came to the plank fence surrounding Chamberlain's backyard. After looking in both directions to make sure he wasn't being observed, he unhooked the latch on the gate and looked inside. His luck was good. No one was in sight.

He checked the windows, which were open to catch any stray breeze to cool the interior of the house. The root cellar was not locked—Hinkle wondered if it had an opening into the basement. The lock on the back door shouldn't be a problem. He left the backyard, shutting the gate behind him. He slinked around the fence line and peered at each window on both sides of the house. Afraid of being observed, he did not go around to the front of the house.

Creeping back to the alley, he resumed his nonchalant manner, whistling an off-key tune as he sauntered back the way he had come. He had good news for John. This job would be a piece of cake.

Sarah emerged from the doorway of the factory, fear making her heart pound as the key turned in the lock behind her.

Moses gripped his stick tightly. "Missus Sarah, is somethin' wrong wif da mista?"

Trying to control her terror, she turned to Moses. "I am afraid that Captain Chamberlain is in terrible danger, and we must get help. I need to apprise Beatrice of the situation immediately." Picking up her plaid skirts, she set out at a dead run for the town homes a few blocks down the street. Moses ran beside her.

Her ankle boots were not made for jogging, much less running, and by the time Sarah arrived at Beatrice's, her feet were protesting the punishment inflicted upon them. Ignoring the pain, Sarah pounded on the door. Gracie opened it almost immediately, a look of shock on her dark brown face at the sight of Sarah's disheveled appearance and breathing like a winded horse.

Sarah tried to catch her breath as Moses asked for Missus Beatrice. Gracie rushed off, as fast as her substantial frame would allow, to find her mistress. Moses helped Sarah sit in a chair in the parlor.

Beatrice showed up almost instantly, her face a mask of worry. "Oh, good Lord, Sarah, whatever is the matter?"

Still gulping for air, Sarah said, "I need to borrow your buggy straightaway. I must go see the general."

Eyes round with shock, Beatrice clasped her hands together. "General Hartsuff? Whatever for?"

"Robert is in extreme danger. The two guards at the prison think he knows where the Confederate treasury is hidden. I am sore afraid they mean him harm."

Gracie returned with a cranberry-colored glass brimming with water and handed it to her mistress.

Beatrice shoved the glass into Sarah's trembling hands. "Drink this. You look like you are ready to faint."

After gulping the liquid, Sarah handed the glass to Gracie.

Sitting on the settee, Beatrice grasped Sarah's hand. "Now take a deep breath and tell me the whole story."

For the next ten minutes, Sarah told Beatrice everything Robert had told her about the guards, sometimes making a gesture with her free hand to emphasize a point. By the time she finished reporting the most recent conversation with Robert, Sarah had calmed down a bit.

"I understand how worried you are about Robert, but I suggest we heed his advice. Harming or even murdering Robert, God forbid, would be a federal offense. He is under the protection of the garrison, at least until he is paroled. But I am concerned for the safety of you and the young ladies in your care. I will have Jasper prepare the buggy to depart for Richmond in the morning."

Sarah's teeth worried at her lip. "But what of Robert after he is paroled? He will be completely vulnerable once he leaves the prison."

"My manservant Jackson and I will personally pick him up and convey him to Richmond."

Tears forming in her eyes, Sarah smiled at Beatrice. "Whatever would I do without you?"

"If God is willing, we won't have an answer to that for a while."

When a horse whinnied outside, Beatrice took Sarah's hand. "I must go relieve Clarice, who has been sitting with Belle Jefferson. She's ninety and will pass soon, poor soul. All her family has predeceased her, and the benevolent society has been helping out, preparing meals and keeping her company."

"Of course, Beatrice. I will see you tomorrow."

After helping Sarah rise from the chair, Beatrice gave her a hug and walked her to the door. "Now, you go home and have Rachael pack a trunk for you and the young ladies. I will be by in the morning after breakfast to carry you to your sister."

A blister had formed on the heel of Sarah's left foot, and she limped slightly as she climbed the porch stairs. She paused with her hand on the doorknob at the sound of Moses' voice.

"Missus Sarah, don't you worry none 'bout yo' home while you be in Richmon'. Rachael an' I will watch over it."

He stood near the bottom of the porch steps. Sarah looked down on Moses's sweaty, determined face and she had no doubt the place would be in good hands. "Thank you, Moses.

I do not think I could shoulder another burden. Robert is all I can think about right now."

Moses disappeared around the edge of the house as Sarah closed and locked the front door behind her. Rachael appeared at the top of the basement stairs, her smile changing to a frown at the untidy appearance of her mistress. She rushed to Sarah's side. "Missus Sarah, is somethin' amiss?"

Sarah removed her bonnet, shawl, and gloves, and placed them on the hallstand with shaking fingers. Tucking stray blond locks back into her snood, she addressed Rachael. "Something terrible has happened. Moses will apprise you of the details, but I need you to pack a trunk for Abby, Emily Grace, and myself. We shall leave for Richmond on the morrow."

"Yes'm, Missus Sarah."

Rachael hurried to the back door, wrenched it open, and told Moses to bring a trunk down from the attic quickly. Then she turned back to Sarah, who'd gone into the back parlor. "Can I's bring you some tea?"

Sarah collapsed on one of the floral patterned chairs chair. "Yes, please. I have a horrid headache."

As Rachael left, Sarah rubbed her throbbing temples with her slender fingers and thought of Robert. Closing her eyes, she prayed to her Lord for his safety. She tried to comprehend this unfathomably cruel twist of fate.

Rachael returned with medicinal tea, setting the cup on the small wooden table beside Sarah. As she took a sip, Moses returned from the attic and announced that the trunk had been put in Sarah's bedroom.

"Thank you, Moses."

Rachael turned an anxious eye toward Moses and then back to Sarah. "Missus Sarah, if dar be nothin' else you need, I's gonna pack dat trunk now."

"Would you please wake the ladies and send them down to me?"

"Yes'm." Rachael hurried from the room.

Sarah had finished her tea, and her headache had receded to a dull ache, by the time Abby and Emily Grace crossed the threshold of the back parlor. Giving the girls a wavering smile, Sarah asked them to have a seat on the rose settee. Both girls wore worried frowns as they took in Sarah's appearance. Her snood was askew, and stray locks had escaped, framing her stark, white complexion. The skirts of her dress were covered in dust. Abby knew her aunt well; she never entered the house until she had removed the dust from her skirts, much less sat on her furniture in such a condition. Abby's frown deepened; something was terribly wrong. So deep were her thoughts that Abby jerked when her aunt spoke.

"I have distressing news to impart and would prefer not to disclose it to your tender minds, but I must for your own safety."

Em reached for Abby's hand. Abby's fingers grasped Em's in a tight grip.

Leaving nothing out, Sarah disclosed the situation and the location to which they would flee in the morning. Both girls' eyes widened in shock, and neither spoke.

Trying to tuck a stray lock back into the snood, Sarah finally gave up and reached up with both hands, removing the hair net. Her honey-blond hair fell in a silken mass to her shoulders.

"I am so sorry for the inconvenience," Sarah whispered.

Suppressing a cry deep in her throat, Abby let go of Em's hand and rose to envelop her aunt in a tender hug.

Em sat rigid on the settee, still trying to process what Sarah had just shared. She was beginning to believe she must be a magnet for bad luck. First she runs from her home in fear of her life, no evidence having arisen to the contrary. Then she gets knocked unconscious. And now someone may want to kidnap her.

A man's voice in the back of her head said, *"Murphy's Law—what can go wrong will go wrong."* The voice was familiar—where had she heard it before?

"Emily Grace?"

Sarah and Abby stared at her.

Em took a deep breath and exhaled slowly. "I'm fine."

Sarah laid a hand over her heart. "I believe it would be best for us to stay together throughout the evening. Abby, help me lock all the windows on this floor. Robert believes us to be safe until mid-afternoon tomorrow, but we should not take any chances."

Abby and Sarah went to shut the windows, but Em sat unmoving on the sofa. Something was trying to break through the blackness, where her memories used to be. There were no words, just a feeling that something was desperately trying to get through—something she had to remember. Em closed her eyes and banged her fists on her knees. *What is it? God, please help me remember.*

Like a ray of light, a crack formed in the void, and a piece of paper, old and yellowed, appeared in her mind. There was writing on it, but all she could read was a date: June 24, 1865. Almost the same date she had glimpsed at the top of one of the pages in Sarah's diary.

She concentrated so hard on the faint writing that her head felt like it might explode. Try as she might, she couldn't make it out, and the paper vanished back into the recesses of her mind.

When Abby and Sarah returned, Em told her what she'd remembered, including the date. Sarah could shed no light on it. "Today is June twentieth. Saturday will be the twenty-fourth."

"But what could it mean?"

Abby shook her head.

Because of the heat that rose with the windows shut, the ladies took their fans with them to the front porch and sat in the whitewashed rockers.

"I do not believe anyone would try to kidnap us in broad daylight in plain sight of the neighbors." Sarah pushed the rocker back and forth with the toe of her boot.

Rachael brought them cold water from the pump in lead-crystal glasses tinged a soft pink, setting them on small tables between the rockers. As Abby told amusing stories to take her aunt's mind off of Robert, Em concentrated on the date in her head. It meant something; she was sure of it. Was she supposed to be somewhere else on Saturday? Could it have something to do with her family or the boy she dreamed about?

Abby drew her attention back to the conversation when she mentioned that William had come to the house earlier.

"Why did he stop by?" Sarah asked.

"To tell me that he went to the prison this morning. He felt obliged to have a word with the guard who was rude to us outside of Cousin Beatrice's townhouse. William encountered him outside the building. He informed him that he would be called up for disciplinary action if he heard of another incidence of rudeness to us."

Sarah shot up straight in her rocker. "William—why didn't I think of him? We could explain the situation to him. He would move heaven and earth to protect you, Abby—possibly have the guards replaced, or at the very least, threaten them with prison if Robert or his family is harmed."

The rocker creaked as Sarah pushed to her feet. "I will have Moses run to Beatrice's for the—" Sarah shook her head. "Oh, dear. Beatrice has taken the buggy to Belle Jefferson's home. She could be there for hours."

Abby peered up at her aunt. "We could stop by the Bolling Estate and talk to William before we proceed to Richmond in the morning."

Sarah resumed her seat in the rocker. "Yes, that is a good idea. It would ease my fears quite a bit to know William is watching out for Robert."

Sarah closed her eyes and continued rocking the chair with the sole of her shoe until Rachael called them to the table to partake of a delicious-smelling soup made of vegetables and the bone of the recently acquired ham.

Lying beside Abby in their bed, Em had barely closed her eyes when the window was suddenly lit by a bolt of lightning, followed by a loud clap of thunder. Both girls jerked up and screamed. A strong gust of wind pushed through the window, blowing the mosquito netting apart. Abby and Em clutched each other as another bolt of lightning lit up the room, thunder coming swiftly on its heels. When a third bolt was followed immediately by a boom so loud they felt the house vibrate, both girls dove under the covers for safety.

Rain pummeled the roof. Abby threw off the covers and shouted to Em to help her shut the windows. Em almost slipped and fell in the puddle under the window she was struggling to close. Rain pelted her nightgown as she pushed with all her might on the stubborn window. Abby joined her, using the heel of her hand on the lower part of the frame, finally shutting it. By the time all the windows were down, their nightgowns were soaked.

Abby looked at the water dripping from the hem of her gown. "I guess we had better remove these wet garments and sleep in our drawers and chemises tonight."

The girls removed their nightgowns, letting them lie on the floor so as not to ruin the furniture. Afraid she would step on the soggy mess if she had to use the potty chair during the night, Em shoved her gown under the bed with her foot, never realizing the nightgown was now a mere inch from the diary she had brought from another century.

Sheets of rain poured down the window panes as Abby and Em climbed back into their bed.

"Moses must be thrilled," Em said. "His garden is certainly getting a good soaking."

"Hopefully Moses is not also." Abby sighed. "He was sleeping out on the back lawn tonight to keep an eye out for those guards."

"But he'd go in the house during a deluge like this, wouldn't he?"

"I am quite certain he would."

Em turned toward Abby, able to make out her features by the periodic flashes of lightning. "Do you think we will be safe in Richmond?"

"Yes. Once Uncle Robert is freed, he will expose the extortion plot, and the guards will be arrested."

"But they could try to kill him before he is released."

"William will not let that happen. When we apprise him of the graveness of the situation, he will have the guards taken into custody."

Em clutched at the bedcovers. "But he works for the general. What if the general is not convinced?"

"The general trusts his judgment. William told me that when Robert was brought to Petersburg after he was captured with President Davis's entourage, the general spoke with him for more than an hour before he was brought to the prison. The general told William that he believed Robert to be a fair and honest man and that he respected him, despite the fact that they were on opposite sides during the war."

Abby patted Em's shoulder. "Rest easy, Emily Grace. Everything will be fine."

Em rolled onto her stomach, not feeling reassured. She had a bad feeling deep in her bones that wouldn't go away no matter what anyone said.

Chapter Thirteen

June 21, 1865

Breakfast was subdued as each person at the dining room table pondered her own thoughts. Em glanced out a nearby window, staring at the glistening drops from the previous night's rain drip off the green leaves of a nearby maple tree. Anxiety tore at her as she thought about leaving Petersburg. She felt sure that her best chance of remembering who she was lay in this city where she could encounter something or someone to trigger her memory. Closing her eyes, she sent a plea heavenward. *Please, Lord, help William to put the guards in jail so we can return to Petersburg soon.*

"Emily Grace, would you care for another slice of gingerbread?" Sarah pushed the platter closer to Em's reach.

"Thank you." Em took a piece and nibbled off a corner.

"I, declare, Emily Grace, your eyes look a million miles away. Are you wool-gathering?"

Startled, Em looked up, but instead of Sarah, she saw a woman with pretty auburn hair. "My mother!"

"Did you remember something about her?" Abby asked.

"Yes. I just had a vision of us together. She was saying the same phrase Sarah just used: *wool-gathering.*"

"Is there anything else?"

Em concentrated, but couldn't come up with more. "It's so frustrating. All I get are brief flashes."

When a knock came on the front door, all three glanced to the hallway. Sarah went to the door and unlocked it, then welcomed Beatrice with a hug. "Have you had breakfast, dear cousin?"

"I have." Walking into the dining room, Beatrice spied the platter of gingerbread. "But I would not turn down a piece of that gingerbread."

"Please have some. I will inform Moses that he can strap the trunk to the buggy."

"I would suggest we wait an hour or two before traveling, to allow the road to dry a bit. The storm was brief, so it is not too muddy. But with the extra weight, the buggy could bog down if we leave now."

Sarah sat, looking deflated. "Of course. I am certain you are right."

William rose with the dawn, put on his uniform, and ate a hasty breakfast. Then he mounted his Arabian to join General Hartsuff on a ride to Richmond for a meeting with a military attaché from Washington. President Johnson wanted them to give a full report on the reconstruction efforts in the city of Petersburg.

Large clumps of red clay flew from the horses' hooves as they drew closer to the damaged, redbrick commercial buildings of the city. Sooty vapors arose from large, coal-black smokestacks. The riders pulled on the reins to decrease the horses' momentum. Slowing to a trot, the general and William entered the city side by side.

"William, are you certain I cannot change your mind about this request for a transfer? Your career in the military will be greatly enhanced if you join me on this assignment to the capital when we no longer occupy Petersburg." The general lowered the brim of his slouch hat as he scrutinized William.

William stared straight ahead. "I have no doubt you are correct, sir, but I need to expand my horizons beyond the advancement of my career."

The general smiled. "And would those horizons happen to include an attractive Southern lady of good repute?"

William tried to hide a smile. "As a matter of fact, they do, sir."

"I wish you the best of luck in your endeavor, Lieutenant. I will pen a recommendation to the commander of the garrison here in Richmond."

"Thank you, sir. It has been a privilege to serve you."

A companionable silence fell as they headed for the military attachment headquarters in Richmond.

By late morning, Beatrice said that the roads should be dry enough to negotiate. As the ladies settled in the buggy, Rachael handed up a wicker basket with eatables for the trip. Em took it and set it between herself and Abby. A strong breeze pushed up the brim of Em's straw bonnet. Reaching under her chin, she tightened the bow.

"Now, don't you be worryin' 'bout nothin' while you be gone, Missus Sarah," Moses said from the walkway. "Me an' Rachael will be watchin' for dem no-good Yankees."

"I know you will. Thank you both for your loyalty."

With a flick of her wrists, Beatrice set the buggy in motion toward the Bollings' Centre Hill mansion.

Em stared at the destruction of the buildings around her as the buggy jostled over the river stones of Old Street. *Why couldn't she remember any of this?*

Within ten minutes, they had pulled into a circular drive in front of a stately brick mansion. A Union soldier standing on the wide front porch rushed down the stone steps to help Sarah exit the buggy. A strong wind threatened to lift her plaid skirts and expose her ankles.

"Thank you, Sergeant. I am here to see Lieutenant William Hackett."

"I am sorry, ma'am, but the lieutenant left with the general earlier this morning for Richmond. They won't return until this afternoon."

Sarah gripped the edge of the buggy. "This is grievous news. Do you know what time they are expected?"

"No, ma'am, I do not."

"Could I perchance speak with Major Stevens?"

Sergeant Wilson was sorry to have to disappoint the beautiful young woman again. "Ma'am, smoke was sighted west of the city, and the major has gone to investigate."

"And when—"

The city's warning bells shattered the stillness of the morning and sent a flock of crows fleeing from the large oak next to the circular drive. Abby and Em turned on their cushioned seat as a horse and rider came barreling up the drive. Jerking hard on the reins, a soldier of no more than eighteen pulled his steed to an abrupt stop in front of the sergeant.

Breathing hard, he shouted above the siren, "There's a fire 'bout a half-mile wide burning a mile west of town. The winds are blowing the flames toward the city. The major said to alert all able-bodied men to go to the site immediately to stop it before it burns Petersburg to the ground." He took two quick breaths. "He said to appropriate all conveyances for the mission to move men and supplies." The young soldier looked at Beatrice in the buggy. "Begging your pardon, ma'am, but we will need your rig."

Bristling with outrage, Beatrice shouted to be heard. "That is not permissible "We must leave for Richmond without delay."

The sergeant turned to Sarah. "The private here will accompany you and your companions back to your home. I am sorry, but we will require the use of this carriage for the duration of the emergency."

Beatrice huffed as she moved to the middle of the seat. The private entered the buggy and took the reins from her gloved hands. Sergeant Wilson helped Sarah back into the conveyance, apologizing again for the inconvenience.

Sarah grasped the sergeant's sleeve. "It is of the utmost importance that the lieutenant comes to Sarah Chamberlain's house as soon as he returns. Tell him the situation is dire."

"Yes, ma'am—as soon as he arrives and before he dismounts."

"Thank you, Sergeant." Sarah leaned back against the padded leather cushion.

When they arrived back at Sarah's house, the soldier jumped down and helped lift each lady out of the buggy. He walked around to the rear of the carriage, unstrapped the trunk, and set it on the ground.

The private placed two fingers to the rim of his cap. Then he climbed aboard again, briskly turning the horse and heading back toward headquarters.

Beatrice looked at Sarah with sorrowful eyes. "I am so sorry. If I had not delayed our departure, this would not have occurred."

"Dear cousin, it is not your fault, and I am not sorry to be delayed. I would rather be here. But I am concerned for Abby and Emily Grace."

Abby reached across the space between them and grasped Sarah's gloved fingers. "I have no doubt that William will arrive as soon as the sergeant gives him the message. He will waste no time going to the prison to see to Robert's welfare. We will be fine here until he appears."

Beatrice put an arm around Em. "I agree. And I will stay with all of you until such time as William joins us." She winked. "There is safety in numbers."

Her arm still around Em, Beatrice started up the walk. "Well, ladies, time to go arm ourselves. How many fireplace pokers do you have handy, Sarah?"

As the ladies partook of their noontime repast, Rachael entered Abby and Emily Grace's room to finish the tidying she had started before she heard the knocking on the door and rushed down the stairs, surprised to see that the ladies had returned. She was missing one of the girls' nightgowns. Hands on her hips, she tapped her foot in annoyance as she glanced around the room, wondering where it could have gone to.

Striding to the bed, she looked under the frame and found the sopping mess of white cotton. As she grabbed the garment, she noticed something else. She reached farther under the bed. Pulling the object out, she looked at the small, brown book in her hand. She did not know what the letters on the front said, but it looked just like the little book in which the missus wrote, which she called her diary. *Dis must belong to Miz Abby.* After tucking it into the pocket of her skirt, Rachael picked up the wet nightgown to hang on the line outside to dry.

When she entered the dining room, the ladies were laughing over Abby's account of Em trying to put her corset on herself that morning.

"Is dar anythin' you ladies be requiring at dis time?"

Sarah smiled up at Rachael. "You may remove the dishes. We are finished with the meal. It was as delicious as always."

"Yes, ma'am." Rachael removed the little book from her pocket. "Miz Abby, dis mus' be yo' little book. I found it under yo' bed a bit ago."

"It's not mine. I left my diary back in Richmond."

Sarah stared at the leather-bound book. "It looks like my diary. May I see it?"

The moment she saw the small brown book, a loud roar filled Em's ears, accompanied by a sharp pain to her head, followed by dizziness. She emitted a soft groan.

"Emily Grace, are you all right?" asked Beatrice, seated next to her.

Sarah opened the book. On the inside page were the words, *This diary is the property of Sarah Chamberlain.*

"This *is* my diary. But something is wrong." She flipped through the pages. "The paper is all yellowed, and the ink is faded and barely legible." The cover was brittle and cracked. Sarah looked at Abby. "Is it damaged from the storm last night? And how did it get under your bed?"

"I cannot think how that could be. I have never touched your personal things."

Sarah looked at Emily Grace, remembering her interest in her diary a few days prior. She looked to have a guilty countenance with her head bent over, resting in her two hands. "Emily Grace, did you perchance borrow my diary for some reason? I am not angered, merely confused."

Em raised her head and again and looked at the diary. At that moment her head cleared of the pain and vertigo. Memories came flooding back as she recognized the book as the diary she had taken from the attic. A burst of comprehension jarred her. She was in the past—in Sarah's house—the place where she found the diary.

The room started to spin. For a moment, she was sure she would faint.

"Emily Grace?" Beatrice's alarmed voice seemed to recede to a whisper as Em tried to grasp the possibility of something she knew to be impossible.

How did she get here? The last thing she remembered before waking up in this house was scrubbing black heel marks in the kitchen and ranting to God. She had been blaming Him for everything wrong in her life . . . and for allowing Robert to be murdered. *Robert! Oh, God, no!*

Em stood so suddenly, her chair crashed to the floor, making Abby and Sarah jump. Beatrice grabbed at her heart with both hands. Em gripped the edge of the table, her hands shaking. She remembered the date on the last diary entry. June 24, 1865—the day of Robert's funeral. It stated that

Robert died on June 21, 1865. What was today's date? Terror stopped her ability to breathe.

For a few seconds no one in the room moved. The ladies at the table looked like a macabre wax-museum tableau, depicting horror at a nineteenth-century family dinner. Rachael hurried to Em's side and pulled her hands off the table. "Miz Emily Grace, you listen to ole Rachael. You's in some kinda distress. You gots ta breathe, honey chile."

Rachael's words penetrated her shock, and Em gasped for air. Pulling oxygen deep in her lungs, she concentrated on breathing for a few seconds, then turned to Sarah. "Today's date—what is it?"

"June twenty-first," she stammered.

"Are you positive?"

"Yes, Emily Grace, it is the twenty-first," Beatrice affirmed.

"Oh, no!" Glancing at the wall clock above the sideboard, Em noted the time. It was twenty minutes past one. Robert would be killed today at three . . . unless they could prevent it.

She had to get a grip on her fear. There was no time to waste.

Em was positive that God had sent her back in the past to save Robert. She had no doubts now that He was real. Her eyes filled with tears as she realized how much He loved her.

She blinked the tears away. No time for emotion. She had two hours to convince these women she had come from the future to prevent a murder.

Closing her eyes, Em recalled the breathing exercises she always used to calm herself and put her in the zone for a basketball game. Ignoring the voices around her, she took a minute to take deep calming breaths, then finished with a prayer.

Lord, let me be Your instrument in all of my endeavors, and to You be the glory.

The fear and uncertainties that had overwhelmed her disappeared, replaced by self-assurance and feeling of strength only God could provide.

She opened her eyes and looked at Sarah. "This is going to sound strange, but I need you to trust me. Please, go look in your writing table for your diary and bring it back here." Indicating the diary in Sarah's hand, Em continued, "That is not the diary you were writing in a few days ago."

Sarah laid the book in her hands on the table and left the room. When she returned, she held her diary in her hand. Except for looking newer, it was an exact twin to the one on the table.

Sarah stared at Em. "How could there be two?"

"I brought the other one with me when I came here . . . from the future."

Stunned into silence, no one said a word.

"When Moses discovered me in the back parlor, I had just come from *my* time. I thought I was dreaming when the kitchen I had been in changed into a nineteenth-century parlor. When I touched the writing table, I shouted for my mother. Moses showed up with that wicked-looking sickle, and I tripped, hit my head , and forgot who I was. But seeing that diary brought my memory back."

Em picked up the book on the table. "I found this hidden in a secret hiding place in the attic of this house in the year 2008."

All three ladies gasped.

Understanding that Emily Grace had clearly lost her faculties, Beatrice spoke to her in a soothing voice. "Now, child, you are very upset. I believe you have suffered some kind of seizure. Perhaps you should rest."

"If we don't come up with some sort of plan, Robert is going to be murdered in two hours."

The women gasped again.

"It's right here in the diary." Em opened the book to the last entry. She gently took the newer diary from Sarah's trembling fingers and replaced it with the older one.

Sarah looked at the page. "It says *June 24.*"

"Can you make out your writing?"

"It is very faint." Straining to see the words, she read out loud. "I have just returned . . . the funeral . . . must write . . . while I can think . . . overcome with despair. . . . the need for my laudanum and the . . . of sleep. Amelia and Abby hover. . . . concerned . . . . Robert is dead."

Sarah screamed and dropped the book as if it had burned her fingers.

Em retrieved the diary and finished reading the words she could make out. ". . . blows to the head. . . . three o'clock . . . June 21st. The guard said Robert attacked him. I know . . . account is a lie.

Robert told me last week . . . the Confederate gold. . . . that is why he is dead. . . . murdered my Robert.

I must talk to . . . General Hartsuff. If it's the last thing. . . . I will clear my dear husband's name."

Sarah put her hands to her face and wept. Abby rushed to support her. Beatrice sat at the table with an expression of shock and incomprehension.

"Sarah," Em said, "you must stop crying and listen to me. Robert is not dead yet. We can still save him. I believe God sent me here to stop the murder."

Sarah studied Em through tear-filled eyes. She pulled a handkerchief out of her pocket and wiped her eyes and nose. Like a blind woman, she groped for her chair and allowed Abby to help her sit down.

"I believes you, Miz Emily Grace." All eyes turned to Rachael, who set Em's chair aright. "When I was a slave chile growin' up on da plantation, the mistress read da Bible to her chillens an' I listened from da hall. God made dis whole world. Why couldn't He send a white chile back to us to save Mista Robert?"

Sarah looked at the two diaries lying side by side on the table and could come up with no other explanation. She took a deep breath and steeled her spine.

"This is, of course, incomprehensible, but the point is moot. Saving my husband's life is all that matters." The fear in her eyes now replaced with fierce resolve, she explained, "We have to break Robert out of the prison. Knocking on the door at two thirty and visiting until three thirty does not guarantee he won't be killed after I leave."

"I know the reason he is to be murdered," Sarah said. "Robert told the guard he had a friend who would come to the prison by three to apprise him of the whereabouts of the treasury gold. It's not true, but Robert made it up to stall for time."

Beatrice gasped. "If only I had not talked you out of going to see the general." Tears ran down her cheeks.

Sarah gripped Beatrice's hand. "Do not blame yourself. It truly is illogical for Bowers to kill Robert, but the thwarting of his plans must have driven out all sense of self-preservation."

Abby glanced at the clock, and then looked back to Sarah. "How do we break Robert out of prison?"

"We's gonna need Moses. I'll go git him."

Sarah thanked Rachael as she ran from the room. She returned a few moments later with Moses in tow.

Em indicated for them to take chairs at the table. Moses and Rachael shook their heads.

"If you are willing to put your lives in danger to save Robert," Sarah said, "you are part of my family. Please sit with us."

Moses and Rachael sat reluctantly, and Sarah mapped out a plan.

"Before I knock on the door of the factory, I will hide Robert's Enfield rifle behind my back. When Hinkle opens the door, I will lure him out. Then Moses will knock him out with the stick. When Bowers comes to investigate the commotion, I will say that Hinkle tried to accost me and Moses defended me. Before he can react, I will reveal the rifle and threaten to shoot him if he does not let Robert go."

It was a simple plan. But it would require a lot of luck. "How good of a shot are you," Em asked Sarah.

She lowered her gaze. "I admit to having only fired the gun once during a lesson from Robert."

Beatrice shook her head. "We need another man."

"But all the men have gone to fight the fire, except for the very old and infirm," Abby said.

"Do not worry. I can do this," Sarah said. "Neither Bowers nor Hinkle would dare kill me." But her hands trembled.

As Sarah continued to try to allay Beatrice's fears, Abby studied Emily Grace. Gone was the timid, unsure girl. In her place was a confident and fearless young woman.

"I'm an expert shot with a rifle," Em said. When the others gawked at her, she added, "I compete at shooting contests every year in Manassas, Virginia."

The women stared at her in stunned silence.

"I'll go along to the prison and hide behind Moses with the rifle." Before anyone could argue, Em rose from her chair. "Rachael, will you come with me? I need your help."

She and Rachael climbed the stairs to the second floor. After entering Abby's room, Em started to unbutton her dress.

Rachael gaped at her. "What you be doin', Miz Emily Grace?"

"Hurry, Rachael—help me out of these clothes. I have to be able to move fast."

Rachael helped her out of the slips, crinoline, corset, dress, and shoes. From the bottom drawer of the dresser, Em retrieved her clothes. After stripping off the camisole and drawers, Em quickly dressed herself in her panties, bra, blouse, and capris, then slipped her feet into the brown flats. She grabbed her elastic hair band, ripped out the hairpins, gathered her thick, auburn mane into one hand, and deftly looped the band around her tresses.

"Thank you, Rachael." After giving a quick nod to the image in the mirror, Em headed for the stairs.

In the dining room, she found Moses holding a loaded rifle and his stout stick. Abby, Beatrice, and Rachael held wrought-iron pokers.

Everyone gasped at Em's attire. Beatrice, who had not seen her in her contemporary clothes before, demanded to know why she was dressed in her undergarments.

"Rachael will explain after we've gone. Sarah, are you ready?"

"Rachael and I will make sure the house is secure," Abby said with assurance. "We will open the door only to William, whom I will send immediately to the prison."

Sarah glanced at the clock. "It is ten minutes past two. We must hasten to the prison."

Abby closed the door, wishing them Godspeed as the three started down the steps.

Chapter Fourteen

At the McCullough factory, Robert sat on his cot and stared at the pendulum swaying in the clock on the office wall. In forty-five minutes, all hell was going to break loose. The good news was that he only had to deal with Bowers—Hinkle had been called off to fight the fire. The bad news was that he was afraid Bowers would shoot him when his friend did not materialize. He might even get away with it, claiming Robert had attacked him.

Robert got up from the cot. The storm from the night before had turned the interior of the factory into a steam bath. The winds had died down, and only a slight breeze wafted through the iron-barred windows, tinged with the acrid smell of smoke from the fires burning outside the city.

Robert ran his fingers through his damp ebony locks and tried to think of a way to get a jump on Bowers before he blasted a hole in his gut. Striding to the opposite end of the building, he looked for anything he could use as a weapon. It was a futile effort; he had already scanned the room many times with no luck.

A knock on the outside door startled Robert. Afraid it might be Sarah visiting, Robert strode toward the office as Bowers rose from his chair. "If it is my wife, I do not wish to see her."

Bowers stood in the office doorway, his eyes narrow with suspicion. He trained his rifle on Robert. "That ain't your wife. You told her not to visit you today. It had better be your friend with the whereabouts of the gold."

Realizing his mistake, Robert tried to cover himself. "Of course. I forgot about informing Sarah not to come."

A more insistent knock came at the door, followed by Sarah's voice. "Sergeant Hinkle, could you open the door, please? I wish to see my husband."

Fear gripped Robert.

"Well, if it ain't the missus after all," Bowers said. "Maybe we should let her in—keep her around in case your friend don't show up. Yeah, I like that idea. 'Cause if you been lying to me, Hinkle can cart her off to our little hidey hole when he gets back from fire fighting."

"No!" Rage propelled Robert into action, and he rushed Bowers. His rational thinking returned an instant before Bowers pulled the trigger. Robert feinted to the right, hoping the ball would miss him. The bullet plowed into the fleshy part of his hip and exited out the upper region of his buttocks. Searing pain engulfed him, and he staggered.

Robert was vaguely aware of Sarah screaming his name and Bowers coming toward him, the rifle raised above his head like a club.

Having heard rifle fire, Sarah screamed Robert's name again and banged both fists against the factory door. Moses pounded at the door lock with his stick.

Em realized the plan they had formed had flown out the window. And Moses was having no luck breaking the lock. She had to think. She knew this factory. Her history class had visited here on a field trip the year before. An image of a tunnel at the back of the building came to her mind. "Follow me," she yelled. "There's another entrance."

Holding the rifle tight, Em streaked around the left side of the building. Where the brick wall ended, she turned right and found the tunnel. It was only a few yards long and ended in a large iron door. After running down its short length, followed closely by Sarah and Moses, she reached the heavy door. Em could tell that this lock was just as solid as the other one. Despair almost overtook her as Moses and Sarah arrived beside her.

"But it is locked too!" Sarah wailed.

Then an idea came to her from one of her murder-mystery novels. The detective had freed a victim from a locked room by pulling the pins out of the hinges of the door. "Quick, Moses, remove the pins from the hinges."

Moses tugged on the upper pin, but it was wedged in tightly. He banged on it with his stick.

Sarah put her hands together and whispered, "Please, God, allow us to reach Robert in time. Don't let him die."

Yes, God, help us, please. Em prayed.

As Bowers charged him, Robert smashed his fist into the man's stomach, dodging the swinging rifle at the same time. It was like hitting a solid piece of iron. His hand went numb.

An evil smirk on his face, Bowers lifted the rifle for another swing. Blood seeping through his pants from the gunshot wound, Robert timed his next move. As the arc of the rifle swung, Robert grabbed it, kneeing Bowers in the groin at the same time. Bowers doubled over but did not relinquish the rifle. Feeling dizzy and weak, Robert hobbled over to one of the large iron screw presses used to press tobacco. He huddled behind it as Bowers slowly stood, payback time clear in his eyes.

The muscles on Moses's arms bulged as he pulled again on the pin. With a loud screech, it came free. He yanked on the lower pin, and it too slid out. Grasping the bottom hinge in both hands, he strained with all his might. The door scraped open a few inches, leaving a trail of rust on the dirt.

"Just a little bit more," Em shouted.

Grasping the exposed edge of the door, Moses pulled again, and the door gave a few more inches. Sarah rushed through the opening, Em and Moses right behind her. They tore through the cavernous room used to package the pressed tobacco, but pulled up short when another door blocked their way. Sarah pulled on the handle. "It's locked."

Moses easily pulled the pins out of the smaller, lighter wooden door. He yanked it open, slamming it against the wall.

All three froze when they saw Bowers stalking Robert around the iron press, rifle poised to slam his skull.

When Robert's gaze shifted toward his wife, Bowers swung. The butt of the firearm hit him in the side of the head, knocking him to the floor.

"Robert!" Sarah shouted.

Bowers turned. His eyes widened at the sight of Sarah, Moses, and Em.

Sarah hurried to Robert, and Moses rushed Bowers. Both men raised their weapons at the same time, swinging with the strength of arms used for hard physical labor. The weapons collided, resulting in a resounding crack, but neither broke. The men circled each other like boxers in a ring.

Em stared, in stunned disbelief at Robert lying on the ground. *Was he dead or unconscious?* Sarah cradled his head, sobbing.

Lord, Em begged, *please don't let Robert be dead.*

A second crash of the stick and the rifle startled Em back to the present danger. Moses and Bowers had backed up and were circling again, waiting for the other to make a mistake. Both were sweating profusely, but neither took the time to wipe the perspiration out of his eyes.

Hearing a moan, Em looked at Robert. He moved his head slightly.

"Robert, my love!" Sarah exclaimed.

Relief poured through Em's body. But the precarious situation in which they found themselves was far from over. For the first time since arriving at the prison, Em became aware of the rifle she was carrying. Her hands shaking slightly, she brought it to her shoulder and anchored it the way she had been taught. Em prayed that she would not have to use it. If she thought for one moment of the consequences of firing the rifle at a man rather than a target, she wouldn't be able to pull the trigger. And it was a good thing that she didn't pause to think, since they may have all died there in the hot, steamy factory. All of her concentration focused on the life-and-death battle unfolding before her.

Moses was not a street brawler like Bowers and knew none of the dirty tricks he used on the docks. Bowers drew his right arm back as if to swing his rifle at Moses's head. Moses raised his stick to block the attack. At the last second, Bowers brought his rifle under the arc of the stick, then swiftly brought it around, clubbing Moses on the shoulder. Moses staggered under the weight of the blow, giving Bowers the time he needed to kick Moses in the abdomen, sending him hard to the floor. As he raised the rifle again, Em shouted, "Stop! Move one muscle, and I'll shoot."

Bowers smirked at Em. "You ain't gonna shoot me."

Moses was struggling to rise, but having the wind knocked out of him made it difficult. He strode toward Em with evil in his eyes.

"I said stop!"

When Bowers kept coming, Em heard her instructor's words in her head: *"Lower the barrel an inch or two to compensate for the kick, and hold steady."*

She knew she couldn't kill a person. Mentally turning Bowers's chest into a target, she concentrated her aim to the right of the center just below the left shoulder. Taking a deep steadying breath, she pulled the trigger.

Bowers was two yards from the girl when he heard the powder ignite and felt a blow to his shoulder so powerful it knocked him off his feet and the rifle came out of his hand. He hit the floor with a thud. Dazed, he raised his head and looked at the small hole in his dingy shirt. Then he shifted his gaze to the smoke drifting away from the rifle. "The stupid wench shot me." His eyes narrowing to slits, he glared at Em as he tried to rise to his feet. Em eyes widened. She couldn't believe the man was getting up. The rifle in her hand held only one shot.

Having finally gotten his breath back, Moses pulled himself up with the help of the iron press.

A fist pounded on the door and a deep voice demanded entry.

"It is William!" Sarah shouted, still cradling her husband's head in her lap.

"The door's locked," Em yelled. "Go around to the back and through the tunnel. Hurry!"

Bowers staggered to his feet and lunged for Em. Moses grabbed his stick. With his left arm pressed across his gut, he ran for Bowers. Bowers reached out to grab Em, but she dodged left and ran to the opposite end of the room.

Just as Moses raised his stick to strike a blow to the back of Bowers's head, he turned. Bowers reached up with his right hand and grabbed the stick; the two men wrestled. Bowers, proving to be more powerful, wrenched the weapon out of Moses's hand and raised it for a final blow.

A shot rang out. An expression of surprise crossed Bowers's face as he collapsed to the floor.

William lowered his .44-caliber Colt Revolver, returning it to his holster. A grim expression in his blue eyes, he strode over to Bowers. The guard lay face down, unmoving. Using his booted foot, William pushed on Bowers's shoulder, rolling him onto his back. His head flopped to one side, his sightless eyes staring at William's boots.

Em brought a hand to her mouth and briefly closed her eyes.

William's gaze rose from the deceased guard and took in the four people in the room. He hurried over to Robert and

179

Sarah. Kneeling, he examined the wound in Robert's hip. "The ball passed through. Robert, can you hear me?"

He moaned, and his eyes fluttered open. He looked up into Sarah's face and gave her a weak smile. Her tears flowed as she leaned over and gave him a gentle kiss on his forehead.

With adrenaline still pumping through her veins, Em joined Sarah and Robert.

Empathy clear in her voice, she said, "You've got a bump just like the one I had. Your head probably hurts like crazy, but Rachael makes a miracle tea that'll help take the pain away. I just hope you don't lose your memory like I did."

His face grimacing with the pain, Robert looked up at Em. "You . . ." he stammered. "You are in your undergarments."

The stunned look on Robert's face made Em laugh.

"Did that blackguard rip off your clothes?" William said.

He removed his uniform jacket and draped it over Em's shoulders. Em put her arms through the sleeves and buttoned the front.

Another moan from Robert distracted William. "We have to get him to the hospital." With assistance from Moses, William helped Robert to his feet. Draping Robert's arms over their shoulders, they managed to half-drag, half-carry him out of the building and around to the front entrance, lifting him onto the lieutenant's horse. William put his boot in the stirrup and mounted behind him.

He looked down at Sarah. "Once he is cleaned up by the surgeon, I will bring him to your house."

Sergeant Wilson's dappled gray mare thundered up the road towards them. He pulled on the reins, and the horse pranced to a stop beside William. "Begging your pardon, Lieutenant," he said, saluting William, "but General Hartsuff sent me after you in case you were in need of my assistance."

"I am indeed. Sergeant Bowers is dead. Secure the area and arrest Sergeant Hinkle as soon as he returns. I will send someone from mortuary affairs and file a report as soon as I have seen Captain Chamberlain to the surgeon." Pressing his heels into the hindquarters of his black gelding, William set out at a gentle trot, holding his arm tightly across Robert's chest.

As William and Robert disappeared from view, Em began to shake.

Sarah put a comforting arm around her waist. "I would guess that you have never witnessed a man die before."

Sucking in a ragged breath, Em nodded.

"Unfortunately, I have become rather numb to men dying because of my duties at the hospital." Sarah leaned her head against Em's as they walked toward Sarah's house. "Try to put it out of your mind as best you can. I will pray for God to give you peace about the tragedy this day has wrought."

Abby and Beatrice sat in the front porch rockers, alternating between rocking and jumping up to look anxiously up the street toward the prison.

Returning to her rocker after scanning the street, Beatrice moaned, "This is all my fault."

"Please, Cousin, do not blame yourself. Aunt Sarah does not. William is there now, and I am sure he has taken charge."

Beatrice wrung her hands. "But what if he was too late?"

"If Emily Grace was indeed sent to us by God, then all will be well."

"Do you really believe that?"

Catching sight of Moses, Sarah, and Emily Grace, Abby rushed down the porch steps, her shoes crunching on the walkway. She ran up the road, halting in front of her aunt. "Are you all right?" She scanned the road for the two men. "Where are Robert and William?"

Sarah grabbed Abby's hand. "They are fine. Robert had a gunshot wound, and William has taken him to the hospital."

"Robert was shot?"

"Hush, now, darling. We will explain everything in the house."

Abby took Em's hand as the four of them continued up the road to the house, where Rachael had joined Beatrice on the porch.

Chapter Fifteen

Robert returned home, and William joined them for dinner, passing on the news that the fire was under control and Sergeant Hinkle had been arrested. As they ate, Sarah told Robert who Em was and from whence she had come. Even with the evidence of both diaries, he had a hard time accepting this wild tale of time travel.

After the meal, they retired to the back parlor to sip chicory coffee. Robert sipped on Rachael's willow-bark tea. Everyone marveled over the sequence of events that had saved Robert's life.

When Moses and Rachael came in to see if they needed anything, Sarah asked them to join the group. Hesitantly, they entered the room. Sarah rose and walked over to the couple. She reached up and planted a kiss on Moses's cheek. "You saved my husband's life today, which no amount of money can repay. But Robert and I wish for you to accept this small token of our esteem for you." Gently taking Moses's hand, Sarah laid a gold coin in his palm.

Moses's eyes became huge.

"Missus Sarah," Rachael exclaimed, "dat be one of yo' precious coins for da expenses."

Sarah smiled and gave Rachael a hug. "Do not worry your head over it. It is a thank-you gift; do with it as you like."

Em, once again dressed in her nineteenth-century clothes, pushed up from her chair and strode over to Moses. "May I see that coin?"

Moses handed it to her, and Em examined it. On the front was the head of Lady Liberty, wearing a feathered headdress. Flipping it over, Em observed a mintmark below a laurel wreath. It looked exactly like the three-dollar gold coin she had seen on the Internet, when she was researching old coins.

"If I just had one of these in my time, it might save my aunt's house."

"What do you mean, Emily Grace?" Abby asked.

"My Aunt Katy owns the old Fork Inn in Sutherland. Her husband died, and she owes a lot of money from repairs on the house and medical school loans." She took a deep breath. "This coin in my time is worth thousands of dollars. It would pay all of my aunt's bills."

There was a collective gasp as Em gave the coin back to Moses.

"How do you know this, Emily Grace?" William asked.

Realizing no one here could grasp the concept of the Internet, Em said, "Because of the diary, I did research at the library on the time period."

Sarah looked at Em. "Did you say the Fork Inn?"

"It isn't an inn in my time—just a family home."

Sarah continued, "And you said your aunt's husband died, and she owes a lot of money?"

"Yes, ma'am," Em sighed again.

Sarah's smile lit up her whole face. She dipped her hand into the pocket of her dress, pulled out another three-dollar coin, and offered it to Em. "I would guess this coin might be helpful when you return to your time."

"Are you serious?" Em squealed with joy.

Beatrice's forehead furrowed. "Does she think you to be disingenuous?"

Abby giggled. "It's just an expression. It means she is over the moon with delight."

Grasping the coin tightly in her fingers, Em gazed at Sarah. "You have no idea what this will mean to my family." She suddenly realized that first she had to get back to her time. "But I don't know when God will send me back. Or even if he will."

Sarah tipped up her chin with a gentle finger. "I have absolutely no doubt that you will be going back. Perhaps this very night, while you're sleeping."

"Do you really think so?"

"God sent you here on a mission. It is finished, and He would want you back in the bosom of your family."

Em laughed at her use of the word *bosom*.

Beatrice stared at her. "You seem to find amusement in that phrase. Why?"

Em tried to control her mirth. "I don't know. We just don't use that word much in my time."

William sat in his chair with a bemused expression on his face as he watched the excitement and happiness unfolding around him. Unlike Robert, he could not deny what his own eyes told him. The older diary came from the future with Emily Grace. Looking at Abby, he grasped her hand and gave it a squeeze. Smiling, she squeezed back.

Em stared at the coin. "Assuming I do get back home, how am I going to explain this coin?"

Sarah smiled. "You already discovered my special hiding place. Put it in the hole when you get back then show your mother your discovery right away."

Em looked around the room at her new friends. If Sarah was right and she went home tonight then she would have to say her goodbyes now. "I am going to miss all of you so much." She hugged Moses and Rachael. He patted her back, but Rachael pulled her close. "I's gonna miss you an' yo' strange ways, sweet honey chile."

"It won't happen in your lifetime, but one day, black folks will eat, work, and live alongside white folks." Her heart lightened with a sudden thought. "As a matter of fact, in my time, a black man is campaigning for president of the United States."

Moses shook his large head. "Ain't dat somethin'?"

Em walked to Williams' chair, and he rose to meet her. Not sure of how to show her appreciation, she stood for a moment in indecision.

William grasped the hand holding the coin. "It has been my honor and pleasure to have known you, Emily Grace."

"Thank you for saving our lives. I will never forget your bravery."

"Or I yours."

After William let go of Em's hand, Beatrice walked to her side. "Emily Grace, your name will always have special meaning for us. You graced us with your presence and saved our family great pain and sorrow." She chuckled with wry amusement. "I am grateful I did not have a seizure from all the excitement of this day. It was altogether too much for a widow of my advanced years."

"You and me both." Em laughed and the others in the room joined her.

She gathered Em to her ample bosom and held her tightly. After she let go, Em turned to Abby and saw the tears flowing down her cheeks.

Abby rushed to Em and put her arms around her waist and her head against her shoulder. "Selfishly, I do not want you to depart. You have been the sister I never had."

Abby's head barely cleared Em's shoulder, and she could feel the wetness of Abby's tears through her dress.

Em felt an acute sense of impending loss, and her eyes welled up with tears. "I will miss you most of all. Thank you for treating me like your sister even though I was a stranger."

Slowly pulling away, Em looked to Robert and Sarah. Sarah stood beside her husband, seated in the chair beside her, with her arm draped lovingly around his shoulders. Em was struck by how different they looked than what she'd imagined while reading the diary. She gazed at them intently, searing their images in her mind. Robert, so handsome with his gray eyes, coal-black hair, and mustache. Sarah, so beautiful with her fine-boned face, blonde hair, and blue eyes. She would never allow herself to forget.

Robert struggled to rise.

"No, please don't get up," Em exclaimed.

Sarah helped him stand, shouldering part of his weight.

"Gentlemen stand before a lady when they have something of import to disclose," he said. "I am still not sure from whence you came, my dear, but I do know you have saved my life and the lives of Moses and Sarah. My gratitude knows no bounds. Every Sunday in church, I will give an offering and prayer in your name until I breathe no more. Thank you, Emily Grace."

Grasping Em's hand, Robert lifted it to his lips and lightly kissed her knuckles.

Em's heart swelled with the gratitude she felt towards God for allowing her to save Robert's life. "You're welcome."

Robert reached for the arm of the chair and Sarah slowly lowered him to the seat. Then she strode to the writing table and reverently took the old diary into her hand. "I am going to keep this diary so that I may destroy it."

Em gasped.

"You explained at dinner that some of the items in this house are on display to strangers who tour our home in the future. I do not wish for my private thoughts, emotions, and grief of these past five years to be exposed as a curiosity."

Now more than ever in her life, Em longed for history to be preserved. But she also realized that the past was comprised of real people with real feelings that needed to be respected. If she had a diary, would she want someone to read it in a hundred years?

She gazed at Sarah with a wistful smile. "I understand."

"Thank you. Now, no more good-byes. I wish to hear more about the marvelous inventions of the future."

Em returned to her chair, where she described the marvels of the twenty-first century, especially the one she had missed the most in the nineteenth century—the flush toilet.

Em stood in Sarah's bedroom, wistfully looking at the portrait over the fireplace.

"If you wish," Sarah said, "I shall leave it with the house when it is donated to the society."

"Oh, yes, please."

Sarah took Em's hands in hers. "I wish to say a quick prayer." They bowed their heads. "Dear Father in heaven, I thank You this day for Your servant, Emily Grace, whom You have sent. Thank You for Your intervention, which saved my beloved husband's life. Please, Lord, give Emily Grace a safe journey home and bless her with abundant happiness. Amen."

"I don't know how much of that abundant happiness I deserve."

"Whatever do you mean?"

"The last couple of weeks before I came here, I allowed my faith to slip quite a bit. I blamed God for everything wrong in my life."

Sarah squeezed the hands she held. "Our God is forever understanding and forgiving. You will always be His precious child."

Tears welled in Em's eyes. "I will miss you so much."

Sarah lifted a silky lock of auburn hair off of Em's shoulder. "It never would have occurred to me that my angel would have red hair and a freckled face." Sarah smiled. "In all the paintings, they seem to be adorned with blonde hair."

Em felt her face flush. "I'm no angel—just ask my brother."

"You always will be to me." Sarah smoothed the lock of hair. "Now I must go and bring Robert up here to get a good night's slumber."

Em brushed a tear off her cheek. "I love you, Sarah."

"And I love you, darling girl." She hugged Em tightly, then hurried from the room.

Em slowly crossed the threshold of Abby's room, where Rachael waited to help her into her nightgown. Once she was down to her drawers and chemise, Em shook her head at the long cotton shift. "If I disappear during the night and show up back in my time in that thing, I'll have a lot of explaining to do."

Rachael smiled. "Yo' mama shore would be confused."

Abby giggled at the image of Em trying to explain the nightgown to her mother.

Em hugged Rachael again and watched her leave the room. After dressing in her underwear, capris, and blouse, Em put the coin in her pocket, pulled her hair back in a ponytail, and slipped on her flats.

"Are you going to sleep with your slippers on?"

"They're shoes in my time. If I go back while I'm asleep, I'll need them."

Both girls brushed their teeth and climbed into bed. Abby snuggled under the covers while Em lay on top.

Abby squeezed Em's hand. "Good night, Emily Grace. If you are gone in the morning, I wish for you a very blessed life."

"And you too, Abby. Don't let William get away."

"Get away? Where is he going?"

Em smiled. "Never mind."

Closing her eyes as she held Abby's hand, Em thought of the movie *The Wizard of* Oz and whispered, "There's no place like home."

Abby yawned and blinked the sleep out of her eyes. Turning over to say "Good morning" to Emily Grace, she faced an empty space where she had lain the night before. A tear slid down her cheek, and she smoothed the cover with her hand. "I will miss you, Emily Grace."

Chapter Sixteen

Em opened her eyes and stared at the washstand across the room. Sighing, she turned to look at Abby, but she wasn't there. The covers weren't even messed up. *The covers!* The quilt underneath her had changed from cream to a multitude of colors. Glancing above her head, she stared at a pristine white canopy. *"I'm back!* Jerking upright, she jumped out of bed and rushed for the door.

"Emily Grace, this isn't funny. Answer me this instant!"

At the sound of her mother's voice, joy coursed through Em's body. She started to open her mouth and shout, "Mom," when she remembered the coin, reached into her pocket, and pulled it out. She knew the last few days were not a dream. But it was good to see the confirmation in her hand.

"Em!"

Em hurried to the attic door. She opened the door and tiptoed up the stairs.

She headed for the front left corner of the attic. Dropping to her knees under the sloping roof, she examined the wooden slats, looking for the right one. Once she found it, she pressed the nail with her thumb. The catch let go, and the wooden slat popped up an inch.

Sarah had explained that Moses, a talented carpenter, built it for her when Robert told her to hide their coins during the war. Lifting the slat higher, she stared into the narrow space, expecting to see only the cloth in which the diary had been wrapped. Her eyes widened at the sight of two bundles that had not been there the week before.

Em lifted them out of the hole. Both were wrapped in a piece of old fabric with a rosebud pattern. The edges of the first bundle had been sewn together. It jingled when Em moved it. Feeling the contents with her fingers, she knew they were coins. Excitement coursed through every vein, but Em paused in the act of pulling apart the threads. It would lend believability to her story if her mom saw this bundle intact.

She opened the other bundle reverently, just as she had the diary a lifetime ago. It held an envelope, two sepia-tone photos, and the diary! Sarah hadn't destroyed it after all.

Em carefully opened the cover and flipped through the pages. The entries were the same until she came to the last one. Instead of Robert's murder, she read:

June 23, 1865

Emily Grace left us yesterday, and we are all bereft. We do miss her so, but know that she is where God needs her to be. Robert is feeling better today, although still favoring his left hip. It will be a few weeks before he is back to normal.

General Hartsuff stopped by with William after the noontime repast. He wished to personally deliver the pardon into Robert's hand and to apologize for the horrid behavior of the soldiers under his command. Sergeant Hinkle will be leaving for twenty years of incarceration at Leavenworth.

William announced that he has been transferred to duty in Richmond, and Abby is beaming with delight. She leaves Saturday for her home. God has given us an extra blessing.

The mayor of Petersburg, and a personal friend, paid a visit today also. He offered Robert an excellent position as the treasurer for the city because of his experience with the treasury in Richmond. Praise God.

Good night, dear diary.

God bless, Emily Grace.

Em brushed tears out of her eyes as she set the diary aside. She lifted the flap of the age-worn envelope and removed a folded piece of stationery. Deciding to save the letter to read after she looked at the pictures, she stuffed the envelope in her pocket and picked up the photographs. The first was a group picture. William and Abby stood in the foreground, dressed in their finery. Slightly behind them were Sarah, Robert, and four strangers. Flipping the picture over, Em spied an inscription: *William and Abby's wedding, June 20, 1866.* Em assumed the four other people to be Abby's parents, grandfather, and brother. She smiled through her tears.

The second picture was of Robert, Sarah, and a baby bundled in Sarah's arms. Turning the picture over, Em read: *Robert, Sarah, and sweet Emily Grace, June 15, 1867.*

Em wiped the tears off of her cheeks as she gazed at the baby. "They named her after me." She traced her finger around the baby's shape.

After laying down the pictures, she unfolded the letter. Discolored with age, Em held the corners gently as she read.

October 30, 1912

Dear Emily Grace,

You have no doubt recently arrived back to your time and feel the same sadness we all did at your departure. I am sure that you are very surprised by this letter, but I made a decision I needed to share with you.

As you know, I destroyed the diary you brought with you. But I changed my mind about the one you have now pulled out of the hiding place. I reread the whole diary a week ago and, with five decades having passed now, I see it in a different light, without the emotions attached.

I wish for you to allow the society to have every-thing in this hole except, of course, this letter to you. I believe it is a good thing for people of your generation to understand how the war years really transpired and not to romanticize it, as is now so common with the younger generation.

As I write this, it is difficult to believe that you will not be born for eighty years, and yet I have not seen you for nearly fifty years. As you have guessed by the date of this letter, I am a very old lady now. My beloved Robert passed last Christmas, but do not mourn, for we had a splendid life together, which would not have happened except for God's intervention and your help.

My Emily Grace has a fine husband and two grown children now. I am a great-grandmother!

Moses and Rachael passed twenty years ago, within two days of each other. They were a beloved part of our family to the end.

Beatrice lived to be ninety-five years old!

Abby and William have four grown children and many grandchildren. She visited with me yesterday, and we spoke of you, as we always do, with fond memories. We laughed together as we recalled some of your phrases.

I will close now because my granddaughter will arrive soon, and I need time to make my way up to the attic.

With fondest memories and profound gratitude,
Sarah Chamberlain

A tear splattered on the letter as Em folded it and placed it in the pocket of her capris with the envelope. Her hand touched the coin. Pulling it out, she set it beside the diary.

"Emily Grace!"

Em jerked and looked across the attic to where her mother stood on the top riser with her hands on her hips.

"Why didn't you answer me? I have been shouting your name and looking for you everywhere." Elisabeth stomped across the floor to Em. "You weren't up here when I checked twenty—" Her eyes narrowed. "What is that stuff beside you?"

When Elisabeth kneeled down, Em grabbed her with both arms, bawling.

"What in the world?" She held Em until she cried herself out.

Em wiped her runny eyes and nose with the edge of her shirt. "I'm sorry, Mom."

Elisabeth stared at her with a concerned expression. Em needed an excuse for her hysterical meltdown. Telling her mother that she'd just returned from the nineteenth century wouldn't cut it.

"I discovered this hiding place and found a gold coin in it." She held it out to her mother. "I know it's valuable, and Aunt Katy needs money."

Elisabeth stared at the coin in Em's palm.

Em handed it to her mom. Puzzled at first, Elisabeth's eyes went wide with shock as she examined the coin more closely.

"Where did you . . . ?"

Em pointed at the moveable slat and the hole beneath.

"How . . . ?"

Em took a deep breath. "I was scrubbing those stupid scuff marks, and I thought I heard a scratching noise upstairs, so I went to investigate. When I got to the attic, it sounded like it was coming from this corner." Em pointed to the wall. "As I moved closer, I must have stepped on the nail that held the slat down. I moved my foot and heard a click. I looked down and saw the slat was raised an inch. So I knelt down and pulled it up, and I found these things inside."

Distracted by the cache before her, Elisabeth never questioned how Em could have heard scratching sounds coming from the attic, while three floors down in the kitchen. Elisabeth picked up the pictures and studied them. After flipping the pictures over, she said, "Why, this is Sarah Chamberlain and her family." She looked back at Em with a frown on her face. "Why didn't you call me before touching these, Em? You know better."

"I know. I just got excited."

Elisabeth patted her hand. "It's okay, honey. I would have felt the same."

"I wish we'd discovered the coin at Aunt Katy's house."

Elisabeth looked thoughtfully at the coin. "This coin may be worth a lot of money. The benevolent society will probably grant you a substantial finder's fee. And you can do whatever you want with that money."

Em grinned. "I already know what I want to do with it."

Her mom laughed and cried at the same time. "I'm very proud of you, honey."

Em pointed to the sack of coins." "There's probably more in that bag. Think we could look inside it?"

"We really shouldn't.

"Please."

Elisabeth lightly pulled on the edges, and the thread fell apart. Elisabeth and Em bumped heads as they both tried to look inside at the same time. They rubbed their heads and then Elisabeth dumped the contents of the sack into her palm. In the dim light from the dormer window, they stared at five three-dollar gold coins nestled in Elisabeth's palm.

Elisabeth moved her lips, but no sound emerged.

"Thank You, Jesus!" Em shouted.

"We have to put it back in the hole for now—except for one coin, which I'll show to your father. He'll find out the legal ramifications of your discovery."

Em and Elisabeth carefully laid the treasure back in the hole and snapped the plank shut. As they rose to their feet, there came a knock at the front door.

Elisabeth put the coin in the pocket of her blue jeans and clasped her arm around Em's waist. Together they went to answer the door.

Elisabeth pulled the front door open and smiled at Megan and a handsome young man she didn't know. Peering over her mother's shoulder, Em grinned broadly at Josh and Megan. In one hand, he held a cup of strawberry cheesecake ice cream with a small wooden spoon embedded in the middle. He extended his other hand toward Elisabeth. "Hello. My name is Josh. I'm a friend of your daughter's."

Elisabeth grasped his hand warmly. "Em has told me about you."

Em groaned. "Mom."

"It's good to meet you, Josh, but I have to run."

"Mrs. Watkins," Megan said, "is it all right if Em rides home with Josh and me? My mom's waiting at the curb."

"Sure. You kids have fun." Elisabeth stepped through the door after Em, pulling it shut and locking it.

As her mother walked down the porch steps, Em looked at Josh and Megan. "What are you two doing here?"

Megan laughed. "You know the old saying: *If Moses won't come to the mountain, then the mountain will come to Moses.*"

"I think that was Mohammed," Em said dryly.

"I know, but I like Moses better."

"Me too." Em felt a brief sadness envelope her at the loss of "her" Moses. She took a deep breath. "Meg, I apologize for my meltdown the other day. I'll be at Bible study next Thursday."

"That's great! You really had me worried."

Josh handed Em the ice cream. Their fingers brushed together, and Em felt the familiar tingle. "You deserve a sweet treat after all that boring cleaning."

Pausing with a small scoopful of the ice cream halfway to her mouth, Em laughed. "*Boring* is not the word I'd use to describe the last few days . . . uh, I mean hours."

"Seriously, what word would you use?" Megan said.

Glancing over Megan's shoulder, Em saw her friend's mom motioning to them. "Guess we'd better be going."

As they hurried down the steps, Josh reached for Em's free hand. She smiled shyly at him. An image came to mind of Abby's face when William grasped her hand. She wondered if her face looked the same.

Em scooped ice cream into her mouth and laughed with her friends as Megan's mom pulled the SUV away from the curb. No one noticed that the clouds had parted just enough for a ray of sunlight to shine through onto the bronze plaque next to the front door. It had been mysteriously altered from the day before. The lettering now read:

THE CHAMBERLAIN HOUSE
*Donated by Sarah Chamberlain to the Petersburg
Ladies Benevolent Society
in loving memory of our guardian angel, Emily Grace*